# Framed

Brianna Johnson

Copyright © 2017

Published by: Elite Professionals Publishing

All rights reserved.

ISBN: 0692928839
ISBN-13: 978-0692928837

Cover Designer: Creative Ankh

# DEDICATION

I dedicate this book to my three

beautiful children. Eli, Shyann,

and Alana I love you all so much.

# CHAPTER ONE

Michael Sims sat in the parking lot of Rocky Creek Falls High School. The school year had come to an end and like all the students, Michael was ready to get his summer started. He had graduated and was more than thankful he didn't have to deal with that awful school anymore. As far as Michael was concerned the only good thing to ever come out of that place was the fact that he was one of the stars on the football team. He had gotten phone calls from several colleges that wanted to pick him up for their football teams. He was excited to play football on a college level. He just wasn't sure which college he would pick, but he still had time to pick one. It was summer and he was happy to be moving on to the next chapter of his life.

Michael rounded the parking lot of the school in his truck. It wasn't much, but it was what he could afford; a green 1999, Ford F150. It was in good shape on the inside, however not so much on the outside. It had rust spots and a few dents he gave it in the past year. Virginia's snow was no joke and the winter's ice added to the problems. Michael planned to run home and change clothes, then pick his girlfriend Ashley up. They were going to get some food and hang out with friends. Michael hoped Ashley's mom, Bethany, wouldn't be there when he got there. She was determined to keep Ashley away from him and he couldn't figure out why. Maybe it was the fact that he smoked pot every once in a while at school. He only got caught once, but in a small town word traveled fast.

Ashley had been his girlfriend for almost two years. She had one more year of school left, so he couldn't help but wonder how they would work out when he left for college. Michael was determined not to stay in Rocky Creek. He had a loving mom he would miss when he left, but she understood his dream of playing football for the pros was now one step closer. She kept telling him to reach for his dreams and by God he was going to, even if that meant he had to leave Ashley behind. Sure he would try to make it work, but he knew long distance relationships rarely ever worked out. He'd debated with breaking it off with Ashley and using the summer to get over it before he went to college. Maybe he would, but at that moment he was going home then meeting up with Ashley and all his friends for the night. He would deal with all the other stuff later.

Showered and changed, Michael went looking for his mom. Their house wasn't big, but it never needed to be. It had always been only him and her that lived there. His dad left when he was only five and he didn't remember much, if anything about him. Michael never seemed to care because he never asked his mom about him. However, she told him all he needed to know when he turned fifteen. His dad, Jack, apparently couldn't handle being a father and wanted to "dip out" as he put it. Michael turned into the kitchen and found his mom making cupcakes. He loved his mother's cupcakes. Somehow she managed to make them perfect every time and he managed to eat all of them in a two day time period.

"Hey, Mom! I'm going out for a little while. Do you need anything from town while I'm out?" Michael turned to the fridge to get a drink for the ride.

She smiled at him for a second. "I don't think so, but it would be nice if you could do me a favor before you run out."

Michael rolled his eyes and waited for her to tell him

what he needed to do. He was beyond ready to go and Ashley was blowing up his phone. He quickly texted Ashley and told her he would be a little late and slipped the phone back into his pocket.

"Can you go get Buster and untangle him from the tree? I would do it, but that big dog wraps his chain around me every time I try to free him."

As Michael headed for the back door, he turned to his mom and gave her a small smile. "Of course I can Mom. I'm going to cut out the back after I break him loose and go see my friends in town. I'll see you when I get home, okay?"

She closed the oven and set the timer. "Okay Michael, but promise me you're not going to hang out with Ashley tonight. Her mom isn't very fond of you and it seems that when you're with Ashley and she finds out, things get bad."

Michael sighed a little knowing he didn't want to argue with his mom, but he never lied to her either. "Yes, Mom she will be there, but I promise it will be okay. Now I have to go, but I'll call when I'm heading home to make sure you don't need anything. Love you Mom!" Michael said as he went out the door to untangle Buster before leaving.

On the way to Ashley's house, he checked his phone to see if she responded to his text. *Huh, that's funny,* he thought. *She hasn't sent anything back. Maybe she's in the shower.* It was a short drive so he decided to stop at the store to give her a few minutes to get ready. Once he left the store, it was only two streets down and a long driveway before he made it to Ashley's house. It was almost five o'clock so they had to hurry if they didn't want to get spotted by Ashley's mom. Bethany usually got home from work around five-thirty. Michael honked the horn and waited a few minutes. She didn't come out of the house, so he tried to call her cell phone. There still was no response. *Maybe she's still getting ready. Do girls listen to music when they got ready for a date or something?* He had no clue about that. What he did know was that he needed to hurry up and get away from that house before Bethany came home or it would be an all out war.

Walking up to the house, Michael couldn't help but feel like something was off. The hairs on the back of his neck stood up when he got to the door and saw it was cracked open. He stood there debating his next move. Should he go in or should he call someone? Maybe Ashley ran outside for something and forgot to shut the door all the way when she came back. Or maybe something was wrong. He couldn't help but think something was wrong. His gut told him to walk away and call someone. He had only been inside the house two times prior and both of those times ended badly, but he needed to know she was okay. He knocked on the door and called out her name. "Ashley?" He waited but there was nothing. He pushed the door open and walked in.

The house was completely silent. Michael looked around before he started up the stairs. He figured she would be in her room. He moved quietly, not knowing what to expect. Once at the top of the stairs, he called for her again, "Ashley, it's me Mike. Where are you?" There still was nothing. He knew something was wrong, because she should have heard him. He looked to his right where Bethany's room was and the door was closed. He continued down the hall, looking at the pictures of Ashley and Bethany that hung on the walls. He turned to the right and spotted Ashley's door.

Michael moved to the door that had a big pink "A" nailed to the door and some girly stickers on it. It was cracked open just a little to let the light shine out into the hall. The hairs on Michael's neck really stood up. He couldn't figure out why he was so nervous. Ashley was probably in the shower and just didn't hear him. He was jumping to conclusions, right? He opened the door and stepped inside.

He looked around her room for a second. Nothing seemed to be out of place. The bed was unmade, some clothes were left on the bed, and a towel was lying on the floor. Posters were on the bright pink walls and pictures of her were here and there. On her nightstand, a clock was flashing five-twenty. Man, he had to find Ashley and leave before her mom came in and things went south.

Walking towards the adjoining bathroom, he stopped in front of her vanity. *Good Lord, how much makeup did she need? She has enough for a whole town.* He knocked on the door to the bathroom and waited to see what he heard. It was quiet; almost too quiet. He pushed open the door slowly, but couldn't go all the way in because something was behind the door. In front of him, he could see a counter with a large mirror. It was fogged up from a recent hot shower. To the right were the toilet and a picture of two kids in overalls and some kind of saying under the picture. He shoved the door a little so he could slide inside the bathroom and move whatever was in the way. Once he was inside and the door closed, Michael's whole life changed. Ashley was lying naked in a pool of blood. Not knowing what to do, Michael dropped to his knees beside her. He saw stab wounds in her chest and a knife on the ground next to her with a bloody towel lying with it. He scooped Ashley up into his arms and started to sob. How? Why? Who? He had so many unanswered questions. Most of all Ashley was gone and he didn't know what to do.

He just sat there and held her as he cried and pushed her hair away from her face.

"Who did this to you Ash? Oh my God, I have to call 911."

Not really wanting to let her go, Michael laid her down and stood up to get his phone out of his pocket. Just as he was about to call, he heard Bethany call out for Ashley. *Shit, she knows I'm here because my truck is in the driveway.* Just then it hit him that she would think he did it. The sound of footsteps was coming up the stairs and Mike's heart began to beat harder. Bethany came into the bathroom and screamed at the sight of Michael standing over Ashley's lifeless body. Michael knew it was going to end badly. She pushed Michael out of the way and kneeled down next to her daughter.

She screamed, "What did you do to my baby? How could you do this?"

Taking a step back, Michael looked Bethany in the eye. "I didn't do anything. I came to get her and found her like this. You can't possibly think I would do this to Ashley?"

It just so happened she did think he did it and so did the cops. Officer Robert Johnson and his partner Officer Jason Briggs stood staring at him, looking him up and down. His light blue shirt, jeans, and his arms were all covered with Ashley's blood. Michael knew it didn't look good, but knew once the evidence came back they would see he didn't do it. *Wouldn't they?*

Officers Johnson and Briggs' talking brought Michael back to reality. "Boy, are you listening? We need you to come with us to the station. Your clothes have to be taken into evidence along with your shoes and phone."

"Are you arresting me?" At that point Michael's blood was boiling. *How could they think I did this?*

Briggs grabbed his arm firmly. "Not yet we're not, but honestly it's looking more and more like you did it. We can talk it all out at the station." Officer Briggs turned his attention to Officer Johnson, "I'll take him in and wait on you at the station."

"Okay, Briggs. I've got to finish getting some statements

here then I'll be down."

With that, Michael was put in the back of a cop car and felt his life fall apart a little more.

*** 

Officer Johnson wished he didn't have to deal with Michael or Ashley's murder. School had just let out for summer and his daughter Brittany, was going out on a date that night. He really wanted to be there to meet the guy and scare the life out of him. However, that wasn't going to happen. Murder didn't happen in their small town. Officer Johnson knew the news of it would quickly spread. The most they got called out for was a break in every once in a while. Most of the time it ended up being an old abandoned house and kids throwing beer bottles at them.

Officer Johnson was torn. Even though they'd taken Michael down to the station, as far as he knew Michael wasn't a bad kid. Brittany went to school with him. He remembered Brittney telling him they hung out at the local Wal-Mart on weekends in the parking lot. It was such a small town the roller skating rink even closed down. He remembered getting called to Rocky Creek Falls High School when Michael got caught smoking pot. It didn't take long for the whole town to find out. That was the only thing he could think of that Michael got in trouble for; but then again everyone had a bad side. Officer Johnson walked by Bethany and went upstairs to talk to the crime scene technician and see what he could find out.

"It looks like she was stabbed with that knife; twice in the chest. More than likely, it was a tall guy. The victim doesn't seem to be that tall, maybe around five feet five inches. I'm guessing the assailant is around six feet tall at least. I can't see any finger prints on the knife. I'll examine her wounds once I get her in the morgue and make sure it's your murder weapon. However, my guess is that it is," the technician, Johnny said.

Officer Johnson couldn't help but wonder if Michael really did it. From his experience he knew it wouldn't end well for Michael. It was looking more and more like he did it. "What's the time of death?"

"My guess would be around four-thirty and five. Rigger still hasn't set in and she didn't need long for her wounds to bleed out. Also, we scraped under her nails to check for any DNA to see if maybe she fought back. I don't think she had enough time to fight back though. I'll send it to the lab to be sure. That's about all I can tell you right now until I get her to the morgue."

"Alright, thank you."

Officer Johnson gave a final condolence to Bethany and then left for the police station. He walked by his desk and saw Officer Briggs waiting for him. "He hasn't changed his story," he stated. "He says he came by to pick Ashley up to hang out with friends around five pm. He walked to the door and she didn't answer when he called out to her. He went in and long story short that's when he said he found her in the bathroom. He claims he never saw anyone else there. It looks like an easy one, Johnson. I think he did it."

They just needed a motive and some evidence to come back and they could nail him.

Officer Johnson for some reason didn't feel like Michael did it, but he dismissed that feeling. "I agree with you, Briggs. For now we wait for Johnny to call with his findings. Until then, I'll read him his rights and let him call a lawyer. Do me a favor, call his mom. Jenny is a good woman and she needs to know what's going on."

Officer Johnson started to walk away when Officer Briggs stopped him. "What's with you, Johnson? Seems like you don't think he did it."

He couldn't help but sigh. "I don't know Briggs. Everything is pointing to him. I guess we wait and see what the evidence says. Until then, let's book him and get out of here for the day."

Officer Johnson walked up to the door of the interrogation room and looked into the window. Michael had his head on the table and seemed to be sobbing. *This day isn't going to end well for anyone,* Officer Johnson thought. He opened the door and Michael popped his head up and looked at him. "Alright Sims, I've got to read you your rights." After Officer Johnson read Michael his rights, he took him to the phone down the hall.

"I'm having Officer Briggs call your mom. Do you have a lawyer or do you want to wait on your mom and have her call one for you?"

Michael looked down at the phone and shook his head. "I know one and I'll give them a call. Then you can take me wherever you need to."

Officer Johnson sat down at his desk while Michael was on the phone. Once Michael got off the phone, he informed Officer Johnson that his lawyer would be there in the morning; which was perfect because by then all the lab results would be in. He placed Michael in a cell for the night and headed back to his desk. Officer Briggs had gone home by then and he was about to do the same. First, he had to place a phone call to the D.A.'s office and let them know they might have to prosecute Michael on murder. It was right at seven pm before he walked out of the office. He wondered how Brittany's date was going. He really wished he could have been there to scare that Jud kid half to death. Brittany was a good kid and he wanted to keep it that way.

\*\*\*

Michael wished it was just a bad dream. The whole situation was bullshit, but there was nothing he could do about any of it. All he could do was sit there until the morning when his lawyer would come and tell them he didn't kill Ashley. Ashley, he missed her already. He still couldn't believe that she was gone. The bigger question was who would kill her? He couldn't even think of one person who didn't like Ashley let alone want to kill her. Michael was sure Bethany was eating up the fact that he was behind bars. She could not stand him so he would never be able to convince her that he didn't kill Ashley. "Think, Mike, think! Who could have done this?" No matter how hard he tried to think of who it could be, he just didn't come up with anyone. Maybe it was because he was in the shit hole of a jail house worried they really might be able to pin the murder on him. His thoughts ran on his mother. He knew she was probably going crazy, not to mention the fact that he promised her it would all be okay before he left earlier that day. Boy was he wrong; dead wrong.

***

The mysterious man waited years for his plan to take place. Finally, it had. Looking at the local newspaper, he frowned a little. The headline read "Local Rocky Creek Falls High School student murdered. Suspect in custody". He hated it, he really did, but he couldn't let his past come back to haunt him. Now he just had to stay in the shit hole of a town for a few more weeks unnoticed and then he could leave. He closed the newspaper and stood up to find his hat for his clever disguise. He had to be sure his entire plan worked out the way it should; so far, so good. Ashley was dead. Not that he really wanted to kill her, but she had to die for everything to work. Now the cops were looking at Michael for killing her.

All he needed now was for him to go to jail and then he could leave town. Michael's eighteenth birthday had passed a few months prior, so he would have to be tried as an adult. *Yes, everything is coming together just perfect.* If anything got messed up then he would go with the back up plans he had in place to get back on track.

The mysterious man headed for the door of his hotel room. Smiling, he cranked his truck and headed into town to get coffee and some food from a local diner. It was the best place to hear gossip. He needed to see if everyone truly believed Michael killed Ashley. Part of him really hated what he had to do to Ashley and Michael, but he had no choice but to frame Michael. He knew too much.

*** 

Sylvia Ross was a great lawyer who had been friends with Michael's mom for years. Michael knew she would be glad to help him out for little to no money. The bad part was that he had high hopes she could get him out of the mess that he had nothing to do with. Looking across the table at Officer Johnson and Officer Briggs, something told Michael that his situation was only going to get worse. Officer Johnson sat down across from him while Officer Briggs stood in the corner. Michael had a feeling it was going to be a bad cop, good cop kind of thing. Sylvia advised him not to say a word; only for him to listen to what they had to say. Officer Johnson threw a file at him with a picture of Ashley naked and bloody the way he found her.

Michael pushed the folder back to him. "I didn't kill Ashley!"

Officer Johnson turned a page in the folder and pointed to some words on the page. "Ashley was stabbed by someone much taller than her. The suspect has to be at least six feet tall. How tall are you, Michael?"

Michael shook his head at Officer Johnson. He knew how tall Michael was. He was just being an asshole.

"I would say he is about six feet. Wouldn't you, Briggs?"

Officer Briggs only smiled at him.

"See kid here is the thing, you were there at the time she died. The only thing you have going for you is there wasn't any prints on the knife found by Ashley's body. The crime scene techs believe whoever killed her used the towel by her body to wipe the prints off the knife. So you see kid, we know you did it. But we just can't figure out why." He scratched his head as if it made him look like he was thinking. "We talked to a few of her friends. They all say she was going to break up with you because you were going off to college. They also said she had eyes for someone else and probably has been seeing him behind your back. So tell me kid, what happened? Did you get mad because she was cheating or mad because she was going to leave you?"

Michael looked over at his lawyer. She gave him a look like they were stuck and couldn't fight that at all. "I didn't kill her and I had no reason to!"

BAM! Officer Johnson slammed his fist down on the table. "You did it and we all know it," he said. "I'll see you in court where I'm going to bury you! You have one chance right now to make a deal with me, but once I walk out of here, the offer is off the table." Michael looked at Sylvia in shock. Were they really doing this? He didn't even do it. Did they really think they could get a jury to believe them?

"Michael, let's just hear what the deal is they are offering," Sylvia said.

Officer Briggs walked over and put both hands on the table to lean on it. "Plead guilty and we will drop the charges down to manslaughter. We don't believe you went there with intent to kill Ashley. We just think maybe y'all got into a fight. You couldn't take it anymore, so you flew off the handle and killed her not meaning to. We will request that you get the minimum sentence of eight years."

Michael's eyes started to water. *You have to be kidding me*, he thought as he sat there. *They have nothing on me, because I didn't do it! They can't really pin this on me, can they?* Michael looked at Sylvia, but before she even spoke, he already had a feeling about what she planned to say. "It's a good deal Michael, but it's up to you." Damn right it was up to him; it was his life. He could feel it slipping out of his hands. Michael looked down at the paper Officer Johnson slid in front of him. If he signed he'd go away for eight years, but if he didn't and the jury found him guilty, then he could go away for life. He sat there for what seemed like hours thinking about what to do. He picked up the pen and slowly signed his life away.

*** 

Michael's trial was the day before so the mysterious man knew there would be coverage in the media and the papers. He walked up to the newspaper stand outside of the local gas station. He put his money in, eagerly grabbed the paper, and walked back to his truck. He tried not to be noticed by anyone, but he almost couldn't contain his excitement as he got in the truck. No one should have known who he was, but he took extra measures just to be sure. He wore a facial mask that was made to fit his face from a girl he slept with in South Carolina, a dark black wig, and a ball cap to help the wig look real. He tossed the newspaper in the passenger seat of the truck and made his way back to his hotel. Once inside the sleaze ball hotel, he put the newspaper on the table and grabbed a beer from the fridge. He sat down and opened the newspaper hoping for the outcome he expected so he could get back to his life. Not that he had much of one, but it would be better if all the shit was behind him.

He flipped open the paper and found the headline,

*Suspect Michael Sims Convicted of Manslaughter.* "What the hell do they mean 'manslaughter'? That little shit was supposed to go away for murder! How could this be?" He skimmed over the first few paragraphs looking to see how long Michael was sentenced for; crossing his fingers it was for life. He knew that with manslaughter it wouldn't be but he still hoped. In the fifth paragraph it read, *Michael Sims sentenced to prison for eight years.* He slammed his fist on the table knocking over his beer. He was so damn mad that he didn't even attempt to pick it up. What was he going to do? *Think, idiot, think!* He got up and walked over to the bed and sat down on the edge. *I will just have to come back when he gets out in eight years and make him go back. I didn't want to have to kill again, but he has to stay in prison forever. Maybe even get the death penalty.*

Feeling a migraine coming on, the mysterious man rubbed the back of his neck. He stood back up. At that moment the thought hit him of how he could make sure Michael went back to prison. *I will kill his bitch of a mother once he gets out. I'll let him have a few weeks, maybe even a month, of freedom while I lurk in the darkness. For now, I will go back to South Carolina and lay low, but I'll be back Mikey Boy.* He grabbed his stuff and headed for the door. Before he walked out, he looked at the beer on the floor. He made a mess there but he vowed to make an even bigger one when he returned.

# CHAPTER TWO
### 8 years later

Michael looked down at the now too small clothes that he managed to squeeze on. His pants wouldn't even button and his shirt fit entirely too snug. He felt like an idiot standing there. Eight years was a long time. However, his age wasn't the only reason his clothes didn't fit anymore. He stood just over six feet with solid muscles. He worked out in the prison gym most of his eight year sentence. He didn't want to be friends with anyone in prison. He just stayed to himself and did his time. He tried not to get into any fights, but it wasn't easy the first few years there. Being small made his life hell. Everyone tried to steal from him or push him around. So he worked out as much as he could to protect himself and it helped a lot. Once everyone saw how big he was, not many people messed with him. Now, he didn't have to worry about any of that at all; he was a free man. He was an eighteen year young adult going in, but he came out a twenty-six year old man. Michael couldn't help but notice that things looked and smelled so much different on the outside. No more muggy, nasty smells and no more fences to look at. He would never ever own a fence in his entire life.

He grabbed his wallet and carried his four sizes too small shoes with him past the last guard. He could see his mom's car waiting for him at the end of the fence. He almost wanted to run but stopped himself so he could enjoy every second of that amazing moment. *FREEDOM!* Michael realized that his mother was already crying and he had not even made it completely out yet. As he continued towards her, he sees someone standing with his mom and life slows him down a little. *Officer Johnson. This should be good. Nice to see that time has made him age badly. I might as well get this over with.*

"Mom!"

She jumped up and hugged him so tight he almost can't breathe. "Michael! Oh my, how I have missed you! Come on, son, let's go home and get you some new clothes! You look so much taller in front of me than behind a glass!" She said excitedly, barely taking a break in between each sentence.

At that moment Officer Johnson cleared his throat to get his attention. "Michael, take this as a nice warning. I am watching you. I don't give out deals a second time, so if you like this side of the glass you better dot your 'i's and cross your 't's. If you make one mistake, I'll be right there waiting to put you right back on the other side of that pretty glass."

Michael snidely ignored Officer Johnson's threat. Little did Officer Johnson know, he not only intended to dot his 'i's and cross his 't's, but he also was going to find who killed Ashley and framed him for it. He had eight years to think about it and he still couldn't figure it out. But he wouldn't stop until he did.

"I'll be seeing you around, officer. Hope you have a good day."

Michael looked at him with a straight face and opened his mom's door to the car and walked around to the passenger side of the car.

"Michael, I have missed you so much," his mom said as she started to cry again.

"Mom, you saw me this morning and also last week," he said with a laugh.

"Michael, you know what I mean. Boy, you listen to me and you listen well. I'm not losing you again so you best keep your ass out of trouble because I will go crazy without you!"

He looked down at his hands. Not only had he thought about Ashley for the past eight years but also about his mom. He hated that he let her down. He broke a solid promise to her and prior to that he had never broken a promise to her. That was one thing he could never forgive himself for over the years. Even though his mom had told him so many times that it was okay. Honestly, it was not okay in his mind. He hated to admit it, but he knew that Ashley was trouble from the beginning. Oh boy, if he had a nickel for every time his mom was right and he was wrong. *Never again.*

"Yes, Mom. I plan to stay far away from any trouble."

He was going to keep his nose clean; for a while anyways. He needed some answers and was prepared to dig for them.

Michael felt eyes on him as he rode through town with his mom. Town hadn't changed much over the years. A new bar sat across from the local diner now and there was a new clothing store; where his mom pulled into. The town was busy though. He never remembered it being that busy when he was growing up.

"Now Michael, you stay in the car and I'll run in and get you a pair of jeans, some shoes, and a shirt. I'll give you some money when you get home so you can buy you some other clothes that will fit you better. I'll be right back." She gently slapped his knee and got out of the car.

Michael was looking over at the store his mom went into when he noticed people on the sidewalk were looking at him. At first he thought it was because of his clothes because he didn't think people would notice him since he had changed so much. Then it hit him that everyone knew his mom; which meant they knew who he was and were staring because the "monster" had gotten out of prison. He smiled a big smile at an older woman, maybe in her fifties and did a slight wave at her. She did a weird head move to make it look like she wasn't looking at him and speed walked off down the sidewalk. *Ha, Ha, Ha.* If he was going to be a freak show, he might as well make the most of it, right?

At that moment his mom got back in the car with a bag in her hand. She put it down and reached over and slapped his arm. He felt like his jaw had hit the floor and his eyes are going to bug out of his head. He started to rub his now burning arm.

"Hey, why'd you do that?" he asked.

With a serious look on her face she said, "Boy, don't play with me. You were trying to scare that woman to death!"

He smiled a little. "Mom, I just smiled and waved. Everyone around here just keeps staring at me, so I was trying to be nice."

A slight smile came across her face. "Yeah right, Michael. I know you better than that."

He dropped the subject and was mostly quiet for the rest of the ride home. He just sat and took in the view of everything he had missed over the past eight years!

*** 

Wow what a crazy day it had been. If Brittany had to look at one more paper about who needed to go to court she was going to pull her hair out. Everything was rush, rush, rush for her over the past few days. Being a lawyer had its

18

ups and downs, and that day was definitely a down kind of day for her. She reached over to grab the phone to let her secretary Taylor know she was leaving for the day. Six o'clock was a late day for her and she was far more than ready to go home. BEEP...BEEP...BEEP...*Hmmmm, why isn't she answering.* As soon as she set the receiver down her door slammed open and in came Taylor like the building was on fire.

"Britt! You are never going to guess what happened today!"

Brittany rolled her eyes, knowing it was probably nothing too serious. "I'm sure I have no idea, Taylor. What happened?"

Taylor ran around Brittany's desk, leaned over to her, and whispered, "He is out today."

She was about to ask who when it hit her; Michael was out. He was never a big deal to Brittany like people thought he would be. Yes, they went to school together, but they never hung out with the same people. She guessed her dad being the one that put him away was the reason she was always supposed to make it a big deal. Well, that and the fact that he was the only murderer they had in their town in well over fifteen years. Honestly, why should she care? She decided to play dumb. "Who is out, Taylor?"

Taylor stood up straight and gave her a shocked expression. "You are the best lawyer in town and you expect me to believe you don't know who I'm talking about?"

Brittany rolled her eyes and started to grab her things. "Okay, so I know who you're talking about, but honestly why is it such a big deal? My dad put who he thought was the killer away and now he did his time and is out. So what?"

Taylor shrugged her shoulders and headed to the door.

"Okay, but Britt from what I hear he looks good! I mean muscled up with tattoos everywhere! Little bit of hard time made him sexy! No more pretty boy."

Taylor was always like a little school girl when it came to men. She loved to look at them even though she had been happily married for five years. Brittany guessed it never hurt to look, but after her latest boyfriend fall out she had stayed clear of men. It had been three years, but she stayed focused on her work and that's all she needed right at the moment. Her dad had given her the settle down speech so many times, that she was ready to lose her mind.

"Well Taylor, I guess that's another piece of eye candy you have to look at in town. The bad boy type was always your thing in school, wasn't it?"

Brittany walked down the hall and headed for the exit. She could feel Taylor close behind her.

"I don't know Britt, maybe he can become your flavor of the week! HA! HA! Wouldn't that be something? I could write a book about that one. Lawyer hooks up with convict her dad put away for eight years. Come on Britt, even you don't think he did it."

Brittany stopped dead in her tracks. "I said I didn't think they had enough evidence to convict him back then but that doesn't mean he didn't do it. And you know I don't have flavors of the week. Hell Taylor, I don't have flavors of the month."

She gave Taylor the opening she was waiting for. "That's my point, Britt! You need a flavor of the week and who better to use as one? A sexy convict!"

Brittany opened the door and walked outside. "I'm going home Taylor. I'll see you Monday."

***

Michael moved toward the front door to open it for his mom to go in first. However, as he opened the door, he saw banners hanging up and his best friend Mark standing in the middle of the room. A few of his mom's friends were there as well. Mainly the ones she always got together with on Friday nights to play poker. His mom loved to gamble and she was damn good at it too. She even lost a friend over it. She beat the woman in a hand of poker and took all her money. She told his mom to never come around her again. Mark ran across the room, shook his hand, and gave him a hug.

"Hey, man! I bet it feels amazing to be out of that rat hole!" Mark had no idea how amazing it was.

Mark was the only friend that came to visit Michael in prison. Every one of his other friends thought he killed Ashley and hated him for it. Mark was the only one who stuck by his side and stood up for him on the outside.

"Dude, you have no idea how great it is. I'm going to run up and change out of these eight year old clothes really quick. Tell Mom I'll be back down in just a second."

Michael ran to his room. He opened the door and he couldn't believe his eyes. Nothing had changed... NOTHING. There were the same posters on the wall, the same bed, the same dresser, the same TV, and even the same mess he left. For a minute, it took him back to being a kid again. He was happy for a short time before Ashley flashed into his mind. The last time he was in this room was when he was getting ready so he could head over and pick her up. He pushed the thoughts out of his head and changed his clothes. It was a happy day for him and he was not going to ruin it thinking of Ashley's death. He had plenty of time to map out his plan later. Today was his freedom day and he planned to enjoy every minute of it.

He went back to the living room where he was

surrounded by his mom's friends; some were crying and others were smiling. They all touched him while they were talking to him, telling him how much he had changed and they knew he was wrongfully convicted. Some also told him stories about his mom while he was away; stories that she probably wouldn't had told him. He looked up and saw his mom smiling from the stories of her added obsession with bingo. Michael excused himself from the group of women and headed over towards his mother.

"Michael, I just can't believe you're finally home. I'm so glad to see you smile. I have missed you more then you know!"

He bent down and hugged her. "Mom, I'm home and not going anywhere. I love you and I've missed you too."

She smiled before she pointed him to the kitchen. "I know you have to be hungry. Go on in the kitchen. Mark is in there making him a plate of food so go on and get you something to eat. Oh and Michael, there is some welcome home beer in the fridge."

He almost ran into the kitchen and passed Mark to open the fridge. Sure enough, there is a twelve pack of beer with a red bow on the top. He reached in and grabbed one out. He popped the top and pulled the neck close to him to sniff it.

"Damn Mike, if that's how you look at beer after eight years, I don't want to see how you look at a woman!" Mark said with a laugh.

Michael gave Mark a go to hell look and took a sip of the beer. *This day couldn't get better,* he thought until he looked over on the counter. *Fried chicken, homemade mashed potatoes, mac and cheese, and corn on the cob.* His mouth watered. *Noodles and PB&J got nothing on this!* Prison food was awful, so that meal was going to be heaven. His momma always knew his favorite thing she made was her chicken.

He made his plate and sat at the table with Mark so they could plan their escape from his mom so they could go hang out.

***

*Back into this shithole of a town. Traffic is terrible; it was never like this back in the day.* The mysterious man pulled up to where his hotel used to be. To his surprise it was gone and replaced by a bar. Great! He headed down to another hotel just on the edge of town. That one was actually better because no one would notice him being there for a long period of time. He got checked in and took his one bag to his room. He was pleased because the place was better than the last one and the price wasn't too bad either.

His timing was right on, because he saw on the news that Michael had been released that day. He would give him some time to get settled in. He didn't want to act too soon or people might suspect something. He would lay back and make sure Michael didn't do anything stupid like try to find him. To be sure, he would follow him from a safe distance. He had enough mask, makeup, and costumes that Michael would never be able to recognize him. He got his first outfit out and got dressed. He was not hungry, but he knew that he would get the best gossip about Michael at the diner.

***

It took a lot of convincing to get Michael's mom to let him go out. Even though he was an adult, she didn't want to lose him again and he understood that. He wanted to embrace his freedom and in a house with walls wasn't the place he wanted to be. Michael slid into Mark's new truck and they head for town.

"Dude, we need to hit a bar and pick up some chicks!" Mark exclaimed.

Michael laughed because Mark had always been a lady's man.

"I would rather stay away from the bars tonight if that's okay with you. Let's head out to the batting cages."

Mark looked at him funny for a second before he pushed the pedal to the floor and headed to the edge of town.

Michael felt better swinging the bat. He needed to get off some built up frustration and it definitely helped. He was so used to being cooped up and working out so much that going almost all day not working out drove him crazy. Mark swung as the ball flew out of the machine. It hit the bat with a loud PING and soared out of the park.

"Dude, I still got it after all these years!"

Michael swung his bat at the last ball and hits it out of the park too.

"Me too! Wait, you don't come here anymore? This used to be your favorite thing to do!"

Mark set his bat down and walked over to the stands.

"No, man. After you got locked up, shit got bad around here. I got into so many fist fights over it. Everyone thought you did it, no one believed you. Well, almost everyone."

"Yeah. You, Mom, and her friends are a small crowd. I'm shocked I even had that many people think I didn't do it."

Michael felt his smile fading fast. He hadn't planned on talking about that type of stuff.

"Yeah and one other person who wasn't at your party," stated Mark.

With sweat running down his back, Michael looked up at Mark puzzled.

"Who are you talking about?"

"Dude, you don't know, do you?"

At that point, Mark stood up with his arms down at his sides.

"Ummm, no Mark I don't know. So, who?"

Mark had a smirk on his face that Michael couldn't help but want to smack off.

"Brittany, dude...Brittany!"

Michael almost choked on his own spit when he swallowed. *Why in the world would the man who put me in prison's daughter think I didn't do it?*

"No way, Mark. That's Johnson's daughter. She would side with her dad one hundred percent."

"Yeah, you would think so right? She's a lawyer now and a few years back her and her dad got into a fight because she told him she thought he didn't have enough evidence to put you away. Boy was her dad pissed about that one. She shrugged it off, telling him it was due to her going to law school. Something about how it was in her nature to look at a case inside and out. But if you ask me, I think there is a little more to the story."

Well it looked like Michael knew who he needed to go see first when he got ready to do his digging. Good old Brittany.

"Can we please head to a little bar and grill at least? I'm dying out here. It's too damn hot," Mark pleaded.

Michael couldn't agree more with him. It felt like if he stayed out there another minute he would melt.

"Yeah. Is Frank's still around?"

"Oh yeah, that place isn't going anywhere. They even have good food now."

Michael wasn't hungry but if the people didn't look at him funny then it might become his new favorite eating place.

"Okay, let's go!"

They got into the truck. Mark looked at him before he pulled off. "So what is the type we are looking for?"

Michael just shook his head. Did he need to find a girl to let off some steam with? Yes, but he really didn't even care. All he could think about was Brittany. They pulled up to Frank's. Michael was happy to see the place wasn't too busy. They sat at the bar and had a few beers talking. The next thing they knew there was a blond girl sitting next to Michael. She might have been twenty-two or twenty-three at the most. She smiled at him and it was over. He knew where the night was going.

Michael woke up on a purple couch and a headache a mile long. He smelled coffee and bacon.

"Hey, glad you're up. There is coffee and bacon and eggs on the table. Eat up."

Michael smiled because he had a great first night home and it started off being a great morning. He got up, got dressed, and headed to the kitchen to eat. The blond was seated in front of him and he had no idea what to say to her.

"Errh...thanks for letting me crash here and thanks for the food."

She took a sip of her coffee and looked at him.

"Oh hush, Hun. I didn't mind at all. I am just glad I could help you. You were wound tighter then a jack in the box!

Prison can do that to you though."

He smiled a little and got back to eating his food quietly. Once he was done, he headed for the door trying to leave without being weird about it.

"Hey, take my number down in case you need me again," she said with a wink. He wrote her number down and walked outside where he found Mark and some girl passed out in his truck. He walked up to the window and yelled "MARK! MARK! WAKE UP!"

Mark jumped up and hit his head on the door. He looked at Michael with an evil look. "Dude, I was sleeping."

"I know dude, but we have to get back. It's after six, and I don't want Mom to worry."

*** 

A few days had passed and people had finally begun to stop staring at him. Trying to find a job seemed to be more of a task than anything. With him having a bad background, no one wants to give him a chance. He needed a job because he refused to keep letting his mom pay for everything, even though she won tons gambling on weekends. He got caught up in the thought about what to do. He came back to reality in time to realize that Brittany Johnson was on the sidewalk staring right at him. He never really had anything to do with her in school, but in that moment all he could think was, *damn how she has changed over the years*. Brittany was always pretty but for some reason he felt like he missed something because the woman who stood in front of him was stunning. Her brown hair hung down past her shoulders. It was straight with just a few waves in it. Her skin tight suit was made to fit her not too skinny, not too big body; while showcasing her long legs. She was amazing. How had he not seen that before in school? *Her eyes are so blue!* He couldn't even look away from them. Then it hit him that his mouth was about to drop open and that he was staring at her like meat on a bone. He was so engulfed in Brittany that he hadn't even noticed the girl next to her whispering in her ear. The girl looked like she was going to jump up and down with excitement while Brittany had a look on her face like a tiger ready to rip someone apart. *Man, she must hate me or something.*

***

Brittany couldn't believe she ran into Michael on her lunch break. Not just any lunch break, but her lunch break with Taylor. She felt like an idiot standing there not even six foot from him staring at him with Taylor in her ear. She didn't have any words come to her mind; she drew a blank for the first time in her life. She was truly speechless! She wasn't sure if she was in shock or if his looks had just taken her by surprise. Though Taylor said he changed and looked really good, she didn't say he looked that good. He was sexy as hell from his brown hair to his rough needing a shave face, to his muscles, and tattoos. Brittany was stuck and couldn't move or speak; she had to think fast. If Taylor saw her looking at him like a piece of meat, she would never let it go. Though she continued to stare, she gave the appearance of a more hardened stare.

"Nice to see you are out, Mr. Sims. I hope you are enjoying the town although not much has changed over the years."

Wow, I sounded like a complete idiot But what did she care? She isn't trying to impress this guy, right?

He looked at her now with a little more solid face. "Yes, Ms. Johnson it is nice to be out. It's also good to see you. I haven't seen you since high school. I hear you're a lawyer now?"

Just then Taylor squeaked out and said, "She is the best

one in town. Too bad you didn't have her to help you back in the day." Brittany gave her a stern look that she wished would make her shut up.

"I'm not sure that would have worked out well, ma'am. Her dad being the one that put me away and all. It would have caused a lot of problems in the family, if you get what I'm saying."

Thank goodness he said it for her because she would have sounded a lot ruder than that. Brittany knew she needed to end the shenanigans and move on before he or Taylor noticed she was losing her stern face over his charming looks.

"Well, Mr. Sims it was nice to see you again, but Taylor and I need to be getting back."

Just as she turned to walk away, Taylor slipped her hand in Brittany's wallet and gave Michael a card. "Here, take this. This is Brittany's card. It has her direct office line on it and even her cell, if you need anything in the future." She smiled at him and then caught up with Brittany.

"Why would you give him my card?" Brittany asked trying to stay calm even though she was so mad she wanted to yell at her.

"Don't try to hide it, Britt. I saw the way you were looking at him and the way he was looking at you. Y'all have some kind of spark there so don't play dumb with me."

Well Taylor was kinda right. Yes, Brittany was attracted to his looks, but that was it. Nothing else and she would never, ever get involved with someone who had been in prison; definitely not someone who her father had put in there. Deep down she still doesn't think he is a murderer, but still. "No Taylor, you're wrong. Way wrong. Drop this subject now. I am starting to get a headache." She didn't say anything more on the matter for the rest of the day. It had been a long day and all she wanted to do was get her work done and go home.

# CHAPTER THREE

Michael was finally able to find a job in town that paid okay money. It was at a factory that shipped car parts to local places in town. His job was boxing up the parts to be shipped. It wasn't the greatest thing but he couldn't really complain being that he had a criminal history. Plus, it would help keep his mom from paying for everything for him. Things started to look up and Michael was happy.

It had been a week since Michael ran into Brittany and he could not stop thinking about her and their encounter. He debated about if he should call her or not. What would he even say though? *Hey, can you help me find who really killed Ashley? Oh and while you're at it, would you like to go out for a drink. Don't worry, we won't tell your dad. We can just act like high school kids and keep it from everyone.* He knew that would never work. Plus, by the way she had looked and acted towards him, he didn't think she would even help him find the real killer. What was he thinking anyway? Her dad was the guy that not only put him in prison but also hated his guts.

Michael devised his plan to clear his name. He knew where he had to go to start digging up dirt on who killed Ashley. He didn't want to go to her, but he had no other option. She was the only one that might be able to give him some information. Michael pulled up to the house not looking forward to getting out. He didn't even know how to start the conversation off. He knew Officer Johnson would be on his ass soon as after the visit, so he had to make the best of the visit.

He walked up the sidewalk and to the front door. Before he could even knock, the door swung open and there she stood...Bethany. Her arms were crossed as she stared at him; not in shock, but almost like she expected him. He was frozen to the porch, not wanting to move. What the hell does he even say? Before he could muster up any words, she looked away from him off in the distance and says "Michael, I knew you would come here sometime. I just didn't know it would be so soon after you got out. What do you want?"

He almost wanted to drop his jaw. He figured she would yell at him, slap him, or just slam the door in his face. Hell, he didn't even think she would answer the damn door.

"I'm here because I didn't kill Ashley and I need to find out who did. I know you never believed me and you probably never will, but I am just asking for a few minutes of your time, please. Please let me ask you some questions."

She stepped back away from the door and headed inside.

"You have five minutes Michael. Then I never want to see your face again."

He followed her just inside the door and stopped. The last time he had been in this house was when he found Ashley on her bathroom floor. He couldn't bring himself to go any further inside. He couldn't understand how Bethany had been able to still live there after it either.

"I just want to go back to that day for a minute. Did you talk to Ashley at all that day?"

Bethany looked over to an arm chair sitting next to the stairs. There used to be a table with a phone and some flowers sitting there. The chair now took its place and

Bethany sat down in it.

"You sound just like the cops. Ashley called me that morning and then again around four-thirty or five that afternoon. The first time she called was while she was in school. She said she was making plans for when she got out of school that day. We got into a little fight because I told her I didn't want her to be hanging out with you that day. I told her that she needed to be single for a while and get through school and that you would be leaving for college or something eventually anyway. Soon enough you would be old news."

She looked up at him with a hint of anger in her eyes. "I never liked you Michael. You were bad news. I knew it then and I know it now. Anyway, the second time I talked to her she called to say she had a bad feeling. Something she couldn't shake. She said she was home and she just didn't feel right being alone. I told her she was fine. It wasn't like she didn't stay home alone all the time because I got off of work every day at five. But you know that," she added with a glare. "I asked her if the door was locked and she said yes and she checked the windows and the back door as well. I told her she was okay," Bethany was almost whispering now. She looked down at the floor and he could tell she was crying.

"Before we hung up, she said she was going to do some homework and then take a shower. She also said that she might be gone before I got home and as you know that was normal for her. I also asked her what reason she had to feel the way she did that day. She only told me when she got home the house seemed different. She said a few of her things were out of place in her room, but that was all. I just pushed it aside and figured it was a teenage thing. I mean kids put stuff down and never remember where they put it. I didn't press the issue and told her she was fine and that it was nothing." Bethany stood up and looked at him with tears running down her face. "That was the last time I spoke to her."

Michael looked down, not knowing what to say. He stayed quiet for a minute and then looked up at her. "Bethany, I am sorry about Ashley but I didn't kill her. I need to know if you saw anything out of place in her room. Was anything missing that you knew of?"

Bethany looked at him again and he knew it was only a matter of time before she blew up at him and made him leave. He had to push her and get some answers or he might never find out who really did this. "I don't even know. I never stepped foot back in her room again. The crime scene people and police told me they cleaned it up. I wouldn't know though. I put a lock on the outside of her door and I never went in. Still to this day, I haven't been in her room." Bethany walked closer, closing the distance they had in the doorway. "Michael, why the hell would it matter what her room looked like?" She began to yell, "You killed my daughter and I can't understand why you are here digging up the past! You are a free man now! There is no reason for you to be here or even speak Ashley's name! I honestly don't know why I even let you in here! Maybe I was hoping for you to finally tell me why you did it! I was hoping for closure to this madness! But here you are still saying you didn't do it! I saw you kneeling over my daughter's dead body, Michael! There was no one else around, no other evidence pointing to anyone being there besides you! So stop trying to get everyone to believe you didn't kill her because everyone knows you did! Now get the hell out of my house and never come back!"

Michael started walking out the door and stopped. He turned and looked at Bethany one more time. "I am sorry Bethany and I'll prove to you I didn't kill her."

Bethany slammed the door behind Michael and he

walked to his truck. It wouldn't be long and she would tell the cops he was here and they would be on his tail. That he knew for sure. He also knew he needed to get into Ashley's room and see if anything was missing or out of place. He needed to look for some sign of who was in that room and killed Ashley. If Ashley said stuff was moved around then he believed what she said. Why would the cops not look into that? Or did they and just not find anything that looked out of place? And what good would it do for him to look at her room either? He was only in her room a few times when they were together. How would he be able to tell what was moved? He didn't know why, but he had a feeling deep down if he got into her room he would find out something that would help him. He had to get in there fast though. Bethany still worked part time so he would just have to break in while she was at work. If he got caught, he would be done for. But if he didn't go in there, he would never know.

***

"That son of a bitch!" The mysterious man had been watching Michael since he got out of prison. At first, he was happy to see him trying to live a normal life. He figured he'd let Michael have a normal life for a few weeks before he made his move; to make Michael look even more like a murderer. *Now this idiot has gone to that girl's mother. Why would he go to her? Didn't she hate him?* Michael went inside so he couldn't hear their conversation from the tree line that he was hiding in. He was only in there a few minutes and she was yelling at him when he came out. From what he could hear it sounded like he was trying to convince her that he didn't kill Ashley. *That dumbass didn't get it back then and he isn't getting it now. No one is going to believe him. My plan was too perfect back then.* The mysterious man smiled as he flashed back to his handy work.

He only had an hour left before Ashley got home so he had to hurry and get into the house. He crept out of the tree line and moved up to the front door. You couldn't see the house from the road, so he knew no one could see him. It only took him a few seconds to get the door unlocked. He quickly lock the door back behind himself and looked around, almost bumping into the phone table by the stairs. *Who the hell puts that right next to the stairs?* he thought as he moved to find Ashley's room.

Once upstairs he easily identified Ashley's door by the "A" on the front of it. He moved to the door and it was locked. *Who the hell lets a kid have a lock on their door?* He pulled out his tools and within seconds he was in her room. *Now, where to hide?* He moved to the closet. *Hmmmm···this closet is way too small and her bed is way too low.*

He couldn't get over how much stuff Ashley had in her room. He picked up some pictures and look at them before he looked at some books on her nightstand. One in particular caught his attention; Ashley's diary. He picked it up and turned the pages to take a peek. Just then he heard the front door open. *Damn, she is home.* He shoved the diary in his coat pocket. *Why is she home so early? I have to hide and fast.* He opened what he assumed was another closet door and instead found a bathroom.

He jumped in the shower and waited to make his move. He heard her come up the stairs and then go back down them. Though the mysterious man was eager to make his move, he reminded himself that he could not move too fast to insure he did not make any mistake. He'd waited too long to put his plan into play to do that.

Hours had passed since he'd heard any movement from Ashley. He checked his watch. *It's almost 5 o'clock.* He just knew that he'd lost his chance and she'd left. As he raised his foot to step out of the shower, he heard footsteps coming up the stairs. He slipped back in the shower to hide again. The door to Ashley's room opened and shut again. *Good, she is in her room.* He could hear talking and got worried for a second. He didn't plan to kill someone else. *What if it's Michael that is with her? This won't work if he is with her. I'll just have to kill them both. I didn't want to kill Michael even though I hate him. I just wanted him to keep quiet. But if I have to kill them both, I will. I can make it look like he killed her then killed himself.* He listened closer and only heard her talking; realizing that she was on the phone. *Perfect! Wait, what is she talking about? Something about things being out of place. Oh no, I didn't lock the door to her room back. Would that really throw her off to think something is wrong and call someone? I have to hurry up.*

"Okay, Mom...Yes, Mom...I checked all the locks. I even checked the window locks...Okay, fine. I'll see you later tonight when I get home."

The door to the bathroom slowly opened and I made my move. Poor thing screamed like she had a heart attack. Lucky for her, she died quickly. *I used the towel to make it look like the little idiot wiped off all his "prints" from the knife. Of course, I had on gloves. I even wore bags over my shoes and head so nothing I had on me would fall off. I even wore a disguise so she wouldn't ever be able to tell anyone who I was if things went south and she somehow lived.*

He reached down and cleaned the knife on the towel she had wrapped around her, walked out of her room, and down the steps to the front door. BEEP! BEEP! A horn blew from outside as he was about to open the door. He cracked the door just enough to see who it is. *Damn, it's Michael. This is bad. I have to get out of here before he comes in and sees me.* The mysterious man crept to the back door and unlocked it. He made his way out the door locking it behind him.

He ran as fast as he could without being seen through the tree line. He didn't stop until he made it back to his car. Out of breath and tired, he took off his gloves and the bags, then placed them in the glove box. *I will throw them out going down the road far away from here,* he thought as he crunk up his car and headed down the road. He couldn't contain his smile as he drove passed the driveway to her house. Bethany sped past him on the main road. It hit him just how perfect his plan had worked out. He didn't even have to wait for anyone to link Michael to the crime. With Bethany coming home, she would find Michael there with her dead daughter. *This is perfect. Michael will go down for murdering her and her mother will be the one to make sure of it.*

# CHAPTER FOUR

Michael hid out in the bushes and watched as Bethany left her house. It felt wrong to him, but what choice did he really have? Michael walked up to the porch and checked the door knob. He knew it was probably locked but he had to check anyway. He pulled out the lock pick kit he had from when he was a kid. He was rusty so it took him a minute to get the door open, but he finally managed to. Once inside, he walked up the stairs. His heart was going a hundred miles per hour. He reached the top of the stairs and couldn't help but feel a sharp stab in his heart. It was all too familiar and he didn't like it at all. Eight years was a long time but it still felt like it was yesterday that he was there. He got to Ashley's door and sure enough there was a big lock on the door. It took fifteen minutes before he finally heard the click he was waiting on. He reached for the door knob and realized he was holding his breath. He had to get a grip. *It's not a big deal. Just get in and look around, then leave.*

Pushing the door open, Michael stepped back in time all over again. Everything in Ashley's room looked just like it did back then. The bed was still unmade with clothes on it, her towel was still lying on the floor just like before, and the vanity was still packed with her makeup. The smell was even the same. Bethany wasn't joking; she hadn't touched anything. There was dust on everything, but he didn't see anything out of place though. He looked everywhere to see if anything jumped out at him; in her drawers, under her bed, and even in her closet. Still, he found nothing that seemed out of place.

Michael paused to regroup. *Why would Ashley tell her mom that things were out of place and then nothing was out of place? Think, Michael think. There has to be something here.* Then it hit him like a brick to the face. *What if it's not something out of place but actually something that is missing? But, what could be missing?* He looked over her room again. When Bethany asked Ashley what exactly made her think something bad was going to happen, she wouldn't give her a definite answer. So what would a teenage girl not want her mom to know she had? He knew that Ashley kept the lock on her door from the time she snuck him into her room. She'd told him they wouldn't get caught because she had a lock on her door and if her mom came in he would have enough time to hide before she would have to unlock it. Man, was she wrong back then. Her mom caught him and Ashley lying in the bed sleeping. He looked over to the bed remembering when they were lying there talking and ended up falling asleep. He smiled a little. He looked over at her table where her clock sat; which the time wasn't showing because it was no longer working.

He kept staring at the table like he was looking for something. *Wait a minute. Didn't she have a book she always kept on her table? Yes! It was a small book and he even made a joke about it that night. She jerked it out of his hand really fast and put it under her pillow. It had to be a diary! That is what was missing. It had to be! It's something she wouldn't want her mom to find out about and it had to be why she wouldn't tell her mom in detail what was out of place. But why would the killer take a diary? That just makes no sense.* Either way, Michael knew it was missing because it definitely was not anywhere in her room. Now that he knew he had to leave. He'd lost track of how long he had been in there and he didn't know when Bethany would be back. He backed out of the room and locked the door back behind him. Then he headed back down the stairs and out the front door, making sure to lock it back behind him as well.

Michael went straight home. Once he got there he grabbed the phone and headed to his room. He couldn't put it all together on his own and he needed help to figure out what to do next. He knew he had to call Brittney. Lying on his bed, he reached over to his nightstand and grabbed the card Taylor gave him. He flipped it through his fingers thinking really hard about calling Brittany. Would she even be willing to help him? He looked around his room towards his window that was above his desk. He noticed it was about halfway open; which was weird because he knew he didn't leave the window open. He also noticed some papers on his desk too. Maybe his mom put them there.

He got up and walked over to the desk thinking maybe he had some mail. He looked down at the envelope. It was a letter with just his name in red ink wrote on it. He reached down and ripped it open. Inside was a note with two words on it. *ASHLEY. JENNY.* Michael didn't even think before he pulled back his arm and threw a punch; not even caring where it landed. Well, it landed right in the drywall. He knew the note was from the killer and he was madder than ever. He wanted to find the person and kill them with his bare hands. The killer not only killed Ashley but was now coming for his mom. He walked back over to his bed and picked up his phone and Brittany's card. It wasn't too late in the day so maybe he could catch her at work. He walked out of his room and went outside to his truck. He didn't want his mom to hear his conversation. He already knew she had to have heard the wall break and would be asking about it soon enough. He didn't have time to explain and he needed to get to Brittany and fast.

He drove to a park not far in town. He found a spot to park his car and dialed Brittany's direct line.

"Brittany Johnson's Law Firm. She is unavailable right now. This is Taylor, her assistant, how can I help you?"

Damn, he didn't want to have everyone know he was trying to get in touch with Brittany. He had a feeling that Taylor would tell everyone he called to speak to Brittany. He needed to talk to her and he was already on the phone, so whatever.

"This is Michael Sims. I need to speak to Brittany please."

Taylor didn't answer for a second and when she finally did her voice changed into a higher squeak. "Mr. Sims, you just missed her. She has left for the day, but if you check the card that I gave you it has her cell number on there. If you don't have the cell number then I can certainly give it to you."

He could feel himself getting annoyed with her already. "No, that's not necessary. I have the number. Thank you though, and Taylor?" He could almost see her smiling through the phone.

"Yes, Mr. Sims?"

In a stern tone, he said "Can you please keep my phone call to her private?"

Michael didn't even wait for her to respond, he just hung up the phone. He dialed Brittany's cell phone number and waited. She finally answered just as he was about to hang up the phone.

"Hello?"

He froze. How could a woman make him so nervous and speechless? "Hi, this is Michael Sims. I was wondering if you could meet me. I need to talk to you and not over the phone." He waited for what seemed like forever for her to answer.

"Okay, Michael. This better be important. You know how bad it would look to see us out in public together? When and where?"

He could understand the reason why she put it like that. "Meet me at the batting cages around eight. I will be in an older truck and there shouldn't be anyone else there. If there is, then call me and we can meet somewhere else."

She sighed. He knew she hated him and didn't want to meet him but at least she was agreeing to do so.

"Fine, I'll see you at eight."

"Thank you. See you then," Michael said before they hung up.

Michael had a few hours before he had to meet Brittany. Before doing so, he needed to go home and think of an excuse to tell his mom for the hole he put in the wall. He left the park and headed home.

***

Brittany couldn't understand what in the world Michael wanted to talk to her about. She didn't know why she was meeting with him. Maybe it was the lawyer part in her. Being a lawyer made her nosey and curious. Right then she was trying to think of any reason she could as to why he would want to meet with her. Why couldn't he just tell her over the phone? It also made her a little nervous about where they were going to meet. However, she couldn't really complain because she did tell him that she didn't want to meet in public. She wasn't worried he would hurt her for some reason though. It was more of the fact of being alone with him that had her head spinning. She of course, could control herself but she was worried that her thoughts would get the best of her and make her start to actually feel something for him. She had to make her mind shut up for once. She didn't understand what was going on because she never had that problem with a man before. She found herself thinking about him at random times during the day, even at work.

Brittany never had a man get into her head the way Michael did. She'd never taken her mind off of work because of a man before that day. Thinking back, she replayed the day in her mind. It was really busy that morning. The phone was going crazy and she had to be in court at lunch time to get the neighborhood drunk out on bail. She knew it wouldn't even be a week and he would be back in jail, but that was what she did best. Brittany got up to file a paper in her filling cabinet when Michael crossed her mind. If she was his lawyer back then, he wouldn't had went to jail at all. Of course, that wouldn't have happened for many reasons. Number one, she was the same age as him and didn't even know what she wanted to go to college for then. Number two, her dad would have lost his mind over it.

Snapping back to reality again, Brittany couldn't help but think of her dad. If he ever found out about her even considering meeting with Michael, her dad would probably freak out. Whatever it was had to be something serious because she had a feeling he didn't like her at all. The day they bumped into each other in town, she could tell he was annoyed with either her or Taylor. He just seemed angry that she was in town at all. Well one thing for sure she had a few hours to grab some food and get home to change before she had to go to the batting cages. She made a mental note to grab her pepper spray. Not because she thought she needed it, but because she felt better when she had it with her.

*** 

*The little asshole had to get my note by now,* the mysterious man thought as he smiled an evil smile. Sitting in his hotel room, he got up and looked out the window. The day was coming to an end and he needed to see what Michael was going to do about the note. Would he go to the cops? No, he knew he wouldn't go to the cops. No one would believe Michael anyway. So far, everything was going good in spite of a few bumps, but it would all work out. He was just going to stay in his hotel that night and then go to Michael's early the next morning. He planned to hide out to see if he could follow him around that day. He figured Michael wouldn't go anywhere that night, knowing that Ashley's killer would be coming for his mom. He closed the blinds on the window and pulled the curtains together so the light wouldn't shine in his room. Then he walked to the mini fridge and grabbed himself a beer. He sat down on the bed, opened his beer, and set it down on the table next to him before he picked up a book out of his bag that was on the floor.

The mysterious man opened the book and flipped through the pages. He had already read the book a million times over the eight years but every now and then he would flip through the pages and get to know the girl he killed eight years ago. He still kept it after all those years because he could never bring himself to get rid of it. He knew he would eventually have to get rid of it though. He looked down at one of the pages and saw where Ashley drew hearts and flowers around Michael's name. *That's it!* He would send the book to Michael. But he would make sure he wrote in the book too. He would leave a little message for Michael in it. Afterwards, he would make sure he cleaned it really good so if Michael did take it to the police there would be no way they could trace it back to him. He decided to wait a few days to get it to him. For now, he needed to rest. He hadn't slept in a few nights. He laid back on the hard bed and closed his eyes. Finally, darkness found him and he fell asleep.

# CHAPTER FIVE

Brittany grabbed herself a burger and fries from the local diner and headed home. Living ten miles from town to most people seemed like a long trip to work every day, but for Brittany the distance between her and town was a relief. Sometimes it felt like she couldn't get far enough away from their small town. Nearing her driveway she passed the little farm across the street from hers.

She turned down her long winding driveway to her two story, three bedroom and two bathroom log cabin. Her house wasn't much, but it was what she always wanted and had worked hard to get. It had a nice little front porch with a swing on one side and flower beds in the yard. To give it an extra country feel, for her last birthday her dad built a little fountain in the yard that went into a small pond.

Once inside of her house, Brittany hurried down the hall to the kitchen. She laid her food and keys on the island and looked at her watch. It was six-thirty, which gave her an hour to shower, eat, and leave by seven-thirty to get to the batting cages before Michael did. Brittany ran up to her bedroom and looked for something comfortable to wear. Her closet had more suits then normal clothes. It wasn't a date at all so she wasn't going to dress like it was. She grabbed a pair of jeans and a plain blue shirt out of her closet.

Brittney walked into her much too big bathroom. When the house was built, she only wanted two things, a big kitchen and a big bathroom. She loved that room the most in her house. Cooking was a wonderful hobby, but pampering herself was an absolute must as far as she was concerned. The focal point of the bathroom was a huge claw foot bathtub. It also housed double sinks and a walk in shower. It had an amazing shower head. Every time she took a shower, she found herself taking way longer than needed.

Once out of the shower and changed, Brittany pulled her wet hair up in a bun and put on a little makeup. She ran down the stairs and looked at the clock over the stove. It was seven o'clock. *Plenty of time to eat my food and leave to meet Michael.* Just the thought of his name sent her mind into a frenzy. She took a deep breath and sat down at the island. *The diner sure could make a great burger,* Brittany thought as she started eating her burger. She remembered working there when she was in high school. The customers were the greatest. Everyone was always so nice and seemed to be in a good mood. Well, except for one customer. He always had a mean look and would never talk to her when he came in. Every day for a month, he came in then all of a sudden stopped. He ordered the same thing every time and would only point to the menu at what he wanted. She was glad when he didn't come back because he gave her a bad feeling. Finishing up her food, she put on her shoes, grabbed her keys, and headed out of the door. She was ready to find out what was so important that Michael had to meet up with her.

*** 

Michael was showered, changed, and ready to go. He grabbed his phone and the note off his desk and placed them in his pocket before he walked down to the kitchen. His mom was in there cleaning up after dinner. Mark was covering for Michael so he could go meet with Brittany without his mother worrying. He also used Mark as an explanation for the hole in the wall. He told his mom he was lifting weights while on the phone with Mark, he got distracted and accidently made a hole in the wall. He told her he would take his first check and fix it.

"Mom, I'm off to hang out with Mark for the night. I'll probably stay at his place and come home in the morning." Michael planned to hang out with Mark and crash at his house after his and Brittany's meeting. He wasn't worried the killer would come for his mom. He had a funny feeling the note was meant to scare him. It didn't. However, it did make him angry and want to find the person who killed Ashley even more.

"Okay, Michael. Just be careful and call me tomorrow sometime." She turned back to cleaning the stove and he took that as his time to leave.

"I will, Mom. I love you. See you tomorrow," he said before he headed to his truck to go meet Brittany.

When he pulled in at the batting cages there was a black Nissan 350z parked in the lot. He pulled his phone out of his pocket and dialed Brittany's number. She answered on the first ring.

"Hello?" With all the bad things going on, her voice had a way of making him relax a little.

"Is that your car in the parking lot?" he asked.

She spoke softly now, "Yes, it is. Do you want me to come to your truck or you to my car?"

He could tell she was nervous about meeting him. Deep down, he hoped it was because she actually liked him. For some reason, he figured it was probably because she was scared of him. "I can come to your car if you want. Whatever makes you comfortable."

She sighed a little and his heart started to speed up. Man

the effect she had on him was crazy.

"That's fine. Just come to my car."

Michael cut the truck off and got out. He walked up to the passenger door of Brittany's car and tapped on the window. Brittany unlocked the door and Michael opened it. He bent down and flashed a smile. "Mind if I sit down?"

She smiled at him and he held his breath. "Well, I thought that was the plan, Michael."

Michael was happy that she was in a joking mood. Maybe the meeting wouldn't go as bad as he thought. He smiled and got into the car. He hated cars. To him they were too small since he was over six feet tall. It was a nice car though. No doubt she paid for it easily. Being a lawyer definitely had its benefits. He shut his door and turned to look at her wishing they had gotten into his old truck. Because the car was small, Brittany was super close to him. It only made his feelings for her grow.

"So, I'm dying to know. What do you need to talk to me about? Did you get into some trouble and need help? With my dad and your relationship, I don't know if I could help much," Brittney said.

"Well, I guess let me start by the usual thing I seem to say; I didn't kill Ashley. I have been working on proving I didn't for the past week or so. I know you probably think I should just leave it alone and maybe you're right. Look at it from my side. I just spent eight years of my life behind bars for something I didn't do. Either way, I need help. I can't do this on my own. I know you probably won't help me. I already figured that before I even called you, but you're my only chance to prove this. I need someone to trust. I don't really have anyone right now and for some reason I feel like I can trust you. Before I tell you anything, can I trust you? Will you at least think about helping me?"

"I don't know what to say," Brittany said after a short pause. "I guess, why me? You should know I won't tell anyone. I couldn't risk anyone finding out we are even talking. I'm just a lawyer, so what do you think I can do to help you?"

*Well, that wasn't a no,* he thought. "Brittany, I honestly don't know how you could help, but I do know that it is worth a try. Just listen to what all has happened and then you can make your decision."

She looked into his eyes. "Okay, I can't promise that I'd help, but I can promise to listen and not tell anyone."

"Okay, so since I got out of prison, I've had this feeling that someone was watching me. I tried to let it go, but now I think I may have been watched. Anyway, I started to think more and more about the day Ashley was killed. I thought about the time of her death and the time I showed up. I'm guessing I got to her house just as the killer murdered her. So, I went back to where it all began. I went and saw Bethany, that's Ashley's mom. I know you are going to tell me it was stupid, but it wasn't. She was calm about me being there at first. She even said she expected me to show up. Anyway, I asked her some questions and in the end she kicked me out. She told me Ashley called her that day and was really freaked out when she got home. Ashley told her mom things were out of place in her room and she had a bad feeling. However, she didn't tell her mom in detail what was out of place and didn't feel right, but it was enough to freak Ashley out. That's all I got out of my visit with her."

Brittany held up her hand to stop him. "Okay, Michael. Let me get this straight. You thought it would be okay to go see the mother of the girl that you were put in prison for killing? Like you said, that was stupid. Do you understand she could have had you put right back in jail?"

He was surprised at what she was saying. It was like she

cared about him for a second. "Yes, that crossed my mind. Look, I had to start somewhere and she was my only shot for answers to things I never had a chance to ask back then." Brittany shook her head as she waited for him to continue. "If you didn't like that part, then you definitely won't like what I did next. Remember, you promised not to tell anyone about anything I tell you?"

She looked at Michael and nodded her head. The bun in her hair started to come undone which made it even harder for Michael not to look at her. He almost couldn't think about what he needed to tell her.

"Bethany said she never, ever went back into Ashley's room after that day. After the crime scene techs and the police got done cleaning up their mess, she put a huge lock on the door and never touched anything." Brittany's face changed now and he knew she had figured out where this story was going.

"So, I went back to Bethany's house the next day and waited for her to leave. Long story short, she was telling the truth. Ashley's door had a huge lock on it and inside the room time stood still for eight long years. She never touched anything and I mean anything. I snooped around her room for a little while and the only thing that looked out of place was some pictures. Then it hit me that Ashley was talking about something missing that was out of place. I remembered she used to keep a diary on her table next to her bed. That would explain why she wouldn't tell her mom in detail what was wrong. I put everything back like it was and locked all the doors and left. There's more-"

Brittany interrupted him then. "You mean you want me to keep the secret that you broke into someone's home and went through her dead daughter's things? I'm a lawyer, Michael! I work for the law! How am I supposed to keep something like that a secret?"

*Well, I guess trusting her is out of the question.* Michael got angry. He didn't trust anyone even before he went to prison and he felt like an idiot to think he could trust Brittany. He reached for the door.

"Fine! Do what you have to do! Sorry I even trusted you. Yeah, maybe you couldn't help me, but damn I thought at least you would listen to me!"

Michael opened his door and started to get out. Brittany grabbed his arm and he almost jerked it away out of reaction, but he didn't.

"Listen, Michael, I won't tell anyone. Get back in and keep talking, please. I'm sorry. It's not every day I hear people confess to something they did. Usually, I defend people saying they didn't do something."

Michael closed the door and turned to look at her. She was still holding his arm and he didn't mind it one bit. He started thinking maybe he was wrong about the fact that she couldn't stand him. She had a softer look in her eyes, almost like she cared about him and really didn't want him to go.

Brittany finally noticed she was still holding his arm and moved her hand away. She looked down and said she was sorry.

"There isn't anything to be sorry for," Michael said as he looked at her.

When Brittany finally looked up, they locked eyes. He could feel something inside him change. He quickly looked away.

"Like I was saying, there is more. I knew Ashley's diary was missing. There is only one person who could have taken it; the killer. I just can't figure out why. Also, today when I got home I went to my room. I was going to call you. When I looked over at my window, I noticed it was half way opened.

I never leave my window open. It's a pet peeve of mine. My mom hardly ever comes in my room, but I was about to just shrug it off when I noticed some papers on my desk. I found this note."

He pulled the note out of his pocket and handed it to Brittany. She looked down at it and you could tell she was confused.

"Who is Jenny?"

He looked her in the eyes and whispered to her, "That's my mom."

Brittany's face went white. "So you think this note is from the killer and he is coming for your mom next?" He could only nod. "Okay, but it just doesn't make sense, Michael. Why would the killer not kill anyone for eight years? Also, why would the killer want Ashley dead and now your mom?"

He was happy to hear her not call him the killer. Maybe she did believe he didn't do it. She would be one of the few.

"I don't know why he killed Ashley and is now after my mom. I don't even know if he is actually going to come after my mom. Maybe he is just trying to scare me. It's not working, if that's his angle. I do know one thing for sure. He hasn't killed in eight years because he wanted everyone to think I killed Ashley. If he would have killed someone else, they would have known I didn't kill her and his cover would be blown."

"Okay, so what do we do now? We have no idea who it is or if he will strike again. We can't go to the cops. There isn't enough for them to look into. Plus, I really don't think they will believe you at all. They will probably think it's just a way for you to try to claim your innocence."

Michael was happy that Brittany used the word "we" as

she spoke about the situation. "I don't know, Brittany. I just know that I have to do something. I can't sit around waiting for whoever it is to come kill my mom. I know somehow that would get pinned on me too. I think whoever the killer is they are trying to frame me again. I just don't know why."

She looked at him almost with hurt in her eyes. "I agree. I think they are trying to frame you again. I'm sure they figured you would get more than eight years."

He knew deep down she was right. "I have thought for the past eight years of who would want Ashley dead and I can't think of anyone."

She looked at him with big eyes like she had an idea come to mind. "That's it, Michael! It's not who wanted to kill Ashley! It's who wanted to frame you. Think about it. Who hates you so bad they would kill people around you just to make sure you went to prison for life? Who would kill the people you care about to watch you hurt?"

He had to think really hard about that one. He knew people who would want to hurt him now, but he couldn't think of anyone eight years ago who would want to hurt him. "I don't know. Back then, I wasn't a bad kid. I never did anything to hurt anyone or make anyone mad. The only person who did hate me was Bethany, but she wouldn't do it for more reasons than one."

They sat in silence for a while, both thinking. Michael looked up at Brittany and she was staring at him.

"What? Did I say something wrong?"

He smiled at her and she smiled back. "No. Sorry, I didn't mean to stare," she said.

Michael had an urge to kiss her. He knew it was wrong, but he couldn't help himself. It could mess up everything, but he knew if he didn't he would regret it. Leaning over, he slid his hand to her face. She looked at him with her big blue eyes. He pulled her to him and kissed her hard. She didn't move away, so he kept going. His heart ran wild. He'd never felt that way before. He pushed his hand to the back of her head above her neck and softly pulled her hair. She moaned. He kept kissing her. He took his time not knowing how long he had before she pulled away.

Brittany put her hand on his chest and he was worried she would push him away. Instead, she rested her hand there. With his other hand, he grabbed her face and pulled her even closer to him. Touching his tongue to her lips, she met his tongue to hers. They kissed passionately for a while. Brittany broke the kiss and sat back in her seat. Neither one of them said a word. Both of them were out of breath and shocked at what happened. Michael felt more than a spark while he kissed her and he was more than happy he did it. Brittany looked up and their eyes locked again.

"I'm not going to say I'm sorry for doing that. I'm very glad I did. I will say I'm sorry I didn't warn you or ask if it was okay. I just knew if I asked, you would have said no. I didn't want to live with the regret of not kissing you. If you never want me to do it again, I won't. I will respect you and respect what you want. But, please let me say that was amazing."

Brittany just sat there staring at him, not saying a word. He sat back in his seat and waited for her to find her words.

"No, that's not it. I was just wrong. I thought you hated me and then this. I'm glad you did it as well."

Wow, he had underestimated her. He was sure she was going to slap him or tell him she never wanted to see him again. He was happy she didn't tell him not to do it again because he fully intended to soon.

Looking down at her hand, she said "Back to what we

were talking about. What are you going to do?"

"I don't know, but I'll figure it out. You should go. It's late and I don't want to keep you. Would it be okay if I see you again? Somewhere other than a car, if that's okay? It doesn't have to be in public."

She looked out her window, not wanting to look at him. "Yes, that would be fine. I'll try to pull some records from when we were in school and do some digging. Maybe I can find something from Ashley's or your past that might help us. I'll call you tomorrow. Even though it's Saturday, I can still access files from home. If you would like, you could come by my house once I get some papers together?"

He was ecstatic that she would let him come to her house. Maybe she was feeling the same thing he was. Or maybe she was just trying to help him out. "Okay, that will work. I'll talk to you tomorrow."

He leaned over and touched her face again. She didn't pull away. He placed a soft kiss on her lips and stroked her face with his finger. Michael couldn't get over how beautiful she was. Pulling his hand away, he got out of the car and walked back to his truck. He waited until she pulled off before leaving.

# CHAPTER SIX

Brittany drove home slowly. Her mind was all over the place. She had just left her meeting with Michael and was speechless. She was glad he kissed her but never thought he felt the way he did about her. She had read him wrong on so many levels. What was she thinking inviting him to her house? What if her dad stopped by? He wouldn't without calling ahead first though. That wasn't the point. Getting involved with Michael was all wrong. What was even more of a shock was their conversation. He was trying to prove he was innocent. She whole heartedly believed him; but it didn't make sense to her for Michael to go through all this to prove he was innocent after he had already been released from prison. He did his time and he didn't need for anyone to believe he didn't do it unless he really didn't do it. Her thoughts moved to the killer and the fact that he could come after Michael or his mom. Brittney didn't know Michael that well but she knew no one deserved to die. *Maybe I could find something in the files about his past,* she thought as she pulled into her driveway.

After a shower and changing into a nightgown and silk robe, she headed downstairs to her spare bedroom that doubled as an office. Turning on the light, she went to her desk and turned on the new Dell laptop Taylor had ordered for her. It was a gift Brittany purchased herself for the business doing so well. While waiting for the computer to start up, she looked around her office. Plaques hung on the wall from college. Playing softball had helped get a free ride to college.

After graduating college early and the top of the class, she opened her own law firm at the age of twenty-five. Having your own law firm was a big step. It helped when the only law firm in town closed due to the owner retiring. She worked really hard to get to the point in her life she was at. People often told her she worked too much, but she didn't care.

A couch was against the wall and a coffee table in front of it with flowers in a vase. She knew how to decorate a room. She loved to make a house feel like a home. It was something she got from her mother. Cancer took Brittany's mother when she was thirteen. It took her faster than anyone expected it to. Brittany spent as much time with her mom as she could before she passed. After she died, her dad never seemed the same. Even after all the years, he never dated anyone. It made her sad to think about it because she wanted her dad to be happy. She even tried to get him to date a few years prior, but he simply said he didn't have time because he was focused on his work too much. Brittany knew it was a lie and he just didn't want to date anyone, but she let it go. She looked back at her computer and logged into the database on her mission to help Michael.

The next few hours were spent looking through files for any and everything. There wasn't much to find and Brittany was about to give up when her screen showed a sealed file; which was weird because with her credentials she should have access to it. She tried her codes again, but again was locked out. It had to be big for her not to be able to get into. *What if this is the key to finding the killer or at least a clue in the right direction?* She looked at her watch thinking about calling Michael. It was midnight and she didn't know if he was still up or not. She had to call him. She went upstairs to her room and got her phone off the bed. Brittany dialed his number and crossed her fingers he would answer.

\*\*\*

Michael thought of Brittany the whole way to Mark's house. He thought of their kiss and how bad he wanted to be with her. He wouldn't allow himself to circum to that desire though because he wanted more than a one night stand with her. He cared about her. So much had gone into that kiss that it was crazy. How could his feelings be that strong when they only spent an hour in a car together? He couldn't explain it but he knew he was going to do everything in his power to make sure he kept that feeling and Brittany around.

He got out of his truck and walked to Mark's door. He rang the bell and waited. Mark lived in a small house on the edge of town. It was definitely a bachelor's pad. It needed a woman's touch mostly because of the smell the house sometimes had. Girls loved his house though. Mark was a lady's man and knew it. He was almost six foot tall with dark hair. Mark came to the door and let Michael in. The minute the door shut, Mark started with the questions. "Okay man, so tell me why you met with Brittany Johnson? And why are you being so weird lately?"

Michael went and sat down in Mark's recliner. He picked up the remote and turned on the TV; making himself at home. "First, I have been acting weird because I'm trying to find out who really killed Ashley. I went to meet with Brittany because I needed her help," he said not wanting to give Mark too many details right out on his situation with finding the killer. He would just keep it simple until he had more evidence.

Mark came over and sat down on the couch in the living room. "So, what did you find out? Do you think you can find out who really killed her?"

"Brittany is willing to help me find who did it but right now we don't really know where to start. She is looking into some things for me though." He looked over at Mark and saw him smiling at him. "What's so funny?"

Mark just kept smiling. "You mean you met with Brittany and just talked?"

Michael knew where the conversation was going. "Well, we sat there and talked for a while. She's going to call me tomorrow and let me know what she finds."

Mark looked at the TV. "Okay, so what else happened? You might not know it, but I saw you sitting in your truck when you pulled in. You had a huge smile on your face. So spit it out! What's up?"

Michael knew he had him so why lie? "Alright, I kissed her. She didn't pull away or kick me out of her car. She actually kissed me back and it was pretty amazing. I don't know, Mark. It was weird. It felt like if I didn't kiss her I would regret it. So I did. I even told her if she didn't want me to do it again, I wouldn't. She never said no."

Mark's mouth looked like it would hit the floor. Michael figured he would be shocked because she was the cop's daughter. "Wow, man. So where do you think this is going? Think it'll be just a fling or something more?"

Michael looked back at the TV again. "I don't know dude, but I don't want just a fling if that helps you understand."

"Well, I'm not sure how it will work out with the situation you guys are in, but hey more power to you. If she is worth it, then it will work itself out."

He was right. Somehow it would work out and Michael just knew it.

"Well dude, I'm going to crash for the night. I have to go help my mom in the morning. Just lock up whenever you leave. There is beer in the fridge if you want some and I have some leftover food too."

Michael laid back in the recliner. "Nah, I'm good man. I'll see you tomorrow sometime."

Mark headed to bed and Michael watched TV for a little while. He didn't really pay attention to what was on. He just sat there thinking of Brittany. It was midnight when he decided to lay down on the couch. He hated Mark's couch. There was an old lady throwing out her couch and Mark said he had to have it. It was awful. Michael could feel every spring in the damn thing. He closed his eyes and that's when his phone rang. He reached over and answered it, not looking at the id.

"Hello?" No one said anything. He pulled the phone away from his ear to see who it was. "Brittany?"

She finally answered. "Michael, I hope I didn't wake you."

He smiled when he heard her voice, "No, I was just watching TV. I couldn't sleep. What's up? Are you okay?"

She cleared her throat. "I'm fine; I just needed to talk to you. I'm not sure you want to talk about it on the phone or not but it's about something I found in your file."

Michael froze. *What did she find? It has to be serious for her to call.* "You're right. We shouldn't talk about it on the phone. It's late so I don't want to bother you by coming over now. Do you want me to wait until tomorrow to come by?" His fingers were crossed as he waited for her to answer. Being with Brittany was way better than lying on Mark's couch.

"I don't think I could sleep even if I wanted to. I have too much on my mind. You can come over if you want."

He smiled at the idea of her not being able to sleep. Was

it because she was not able to stop thinking about him, like he was about her? He hoped it wasn't about what was in his file. "Okay, I'll head over. Where do you live?" She gave him directions to her house. "Okay, Britt, I'll see you soon. Let me just let Mark know I'm heading out."

Michael hung up with Brittany and got up off the couch. He turned to head to Mark's door and almost ran into Mark in the dark. "Dude, are you trying to give me a heart attack?"

Mark laughed. "I heard your phone ring. Off to see Brittany?"

"Yeah, she found something in my file and wants to talk in person. Plus, neither she nor I can sleep. Can you give me your spare key so I don't wake you when I come back?"

Mark smiled and headed off to his room. A second later he came back with the key. "I don't think you will be coming back here for the night, but here it is just in case."

Michael laughed and headed out the door to his truck. Since Mark lived on the edge of town Michael got to Brittany's house a few minutes later. He parked his truck next to her car and walked up on the porch. The door opened the minute he rang the bell. Brittany opened the door and let him in with a red robe wrapped around her and her hair was down now. Michael was stunned by her beauty. Her hair wasn't wet like before. It was dry and had a few waves in it. He couldn't stop looking at her. She was near the wall now next to a table in the hall. Michael couldn't help but move closer to her. He pinned her up against the wall with his body. Both his hands were rested on the wall near each side of her head.

He leaned down and moved the hair away from one of her ears and whispered in her ear, "If you want me to back off all you have to do is say so." She didn't say anything, she just shook her head no. "I'll ask you this time, okay?"

Brittany whispered in a soft cracked voice that he could barely hear. "Okay."

He nibbled on her ear before he asked, "Would it be okay if I kiss you again?"

She moaned in his ear and he took that as a yes. He planted soft kisses from her ear down her neck. Pulling her robe open just a little, he stopped and kissed his way back up to her chin. She moaned a little louder and bowed her back off of the wall. He smiled and ran his hands up her neck to the back of her head. He moved her hair so he could see her face. He looked her in the eyes for a second, before he leaned his body into hers and kissed her hard. She moaned once more when he pushed his bulge against her. He needed her to know how bad he wanted her. He needed her to know what she did to him; her body, her eyes, her voice, and her heart. He took his other hand and rubbed his way down her spine. When he reached her ass, he squeezed it softly. She bucked and moaned again. He broke the kiss. He pulled her hair away from her neck and softly nibbled and kissed his way down to her chest, back up to her neck again. He knew he had to stop or he would get carried away. He moved his hand away from her ass and placed it on her back. Then he let her hair go and moved his hand to her face and kissed her lips softly. He could feel how weak she was. He worried if he stepped back she might fall. He whispered to her. "I'm going to let you go now, okay?" She nodded and stood up.

Michael took a step back but didn't let her go all of the way. Once he knew she was okay, he grabbed her hand. She looked up at him and she looked beat. "Where is your room, Britt?"

She looked at him confused. "Michael, I need to show you what I found."

He knew she was right but rest was more important at that time. She could show him in a few hours after some sleep.

"You can show me in the morning. Britt, I can tell you are tired and need some sleep. Now, where is your room?"

She gave him a stern look. "Don't worry about me. I'll be okay."

He wasn't taking no for an answer. He reached down and picked her up in his arms. "I'll just find it myself then. Don't worry; I'm not going to make any more moves. You need sleep and I'm taking you to your room. It would be easier if you would tell me where it is."

He looked down at her and she smiled. "Okay, Michael, I'll show you. Just put me down please." He set her back down on her feet. Brittany grabbed his hand and led him to the stairs.

When they reached Brittany's room, Michael pulled down the covers and sat next to her. "I'll crash downstairs on the couch, if that's okay?"

"No, that's not okay. I want you to sleep in here."

He smiled at her and reached down with his hand and rubbed her face. "Okay Britt, whatever you want."

He got up and went to the other side. She stopped him before he could get into her bed. "You don't sleep with all your clothes on, Michael. Get comfortable. I know I wouldn't want to sleep with all that on."

Michael started taking his clothes off, with Brittany watching his every move. Once down to his boxers, he put his clothes in a neat pile next to the bed and laid down with Brittany. He pulled her close to him and ran his fingers through her hair until she fell asleep. He laid there for a little while watching her sleep. He had no clue where things would take them, but he liked it thus far. He kissed her head and drifted off to sleep.

# CHAPTER SEVEN

Michael woke up alone in Brittany's bed. The light from the day shined in through the window and Michael jumped up wondering what time it was. He never slept late and where was Brittany? Just then he heard the shower running in the next room. He got up and pulled his pants on and went downstairs looking for the kitchen. Once he found the kitchen he went to the fridge to find something to fix for breakfast; hoping it was still morning. He grabbed some eggs and pancake mix out of the bare fridge and started to cook.

Once the food was done cooking he fixed them each a plate and placed them on the table. He already had coffee ready and poured them each a cup. Then he grabbed some orange juice and placed it on the table along with butter and syrup. He sat down at the table and waited on Brittany to come down the stairs. He sipped his coffee for a minute thinking about the night before. He was happy he stayed with Brittany. She needed the rest and he felt like she wouldn't have gotten any if he wasn't there. He figured that she would have worried herself awake all night.

\*\*\*

Brittany woke up with Michael lying next to her sleeping. That was the best sleep she had gotten in a long time. She wanted to take a shower, but did not want to wake him since he looked like he was sleeping well. She slowly slid out of the hold he had on her and went to the bathroom.

She looked in the mirror and was glad that she didn't look that terrible. She cleaned off her makeup and brushed her teeth as she went and turned on the shower. She wouldn't be long because she wanted to make Michael something to eat. She was hungry and knew he had to be too.

Once she got out of the shower she brushed her hair and walked into her room to find clothes for the day. She noticed the bed empty and got a little worried that he up and left. *Why would he just up and leave?* She scrambled for something to throw on so she could make sure he was still there. Looking over on the side of the bed he slept on she saw some of his stuff in the floor. It was his shirt, phone, wallet, and keys; that was a good sign he hadn't left yet. Just as she pulled some sweat pants on she heard something. She stopped moving so she could listen closely. She heard pots and pans moving around. *He must be in the kitchen looking for food.* She grabbed a shirt, threw it on, and hurried downstairs to the kitchen.

He was drinking what looked to be coffee at the table. He only had pants on, showcasing his chiseled chest. So many things ran through Brittany's mind at that moment. Besides the sexual tension he'd aroused within her, she was so happy he stayed over. More than that, he didn't try to have sex with her. That showed her that he respected her and wanted more from her. She felt something special every time they kissed. She didn't know where things were going but she really liked it at that point. Of course, it scared her a lot but what could she do? If she stopped it before it started she would regret it and never be able to forgive herself. Didn't everyone deserve to be happy? It shouldn't matter who it was with, even if it was someone her dad put away for murder eight years ago. *Ugh, what am I thinking? This could be bad.* She pushed the thought out of her mind because she honestly didn't care. She felt something strong and decided to go for it.

\*\*\*

*What the hell? Where is that bastard?* The mysterious man got to Michael's house at four am that morning and Michael's truck wasn't anywhere to be found. *Why would that idiot be okay with leaving his mom unprotected? Did he not get the note? No, he had to get the note. He didn't take me serious?* The mysterious man was so angry that Michael would just overlook him. He almost wanted to march in Michael's house and kill his mother right then, but he couldn't kill her just in case Michael had an alibi. He had a plan and he needed to stick with it. Michael had to come home sometime. He would stay there, hidden in the bushes, and wait until he did.

\*\*\*

Brittany walked into the kitchen and took Michael's breath away. She had on a brown shirt and a pair of sweat pants. Her hair was down and wet with curls in it. *How did I get so lucky?*

"Good morning. I see you made breakfast. So, you can cook? Any other interesting things you can do?" she asked with a laugh.

Michael loved the way she laughed. It made him almost forget about all the bad going on. "Yes, I can cook. Some things not so good, but at least I try. Sit down and eat. I'm going to get another cup of coffee and join you."

She started to walk past him to the table when he grabbed her arm and pulled her close to him. He looked her in the eyes and kissed her on the cheek. He let her go and went to fill his cup.

They didn't say much at breakfast, just looked up at each other every so often and smiled. Once done with breakfast, they both cleaned off the table and started washing the dishes. Michael got a little water on his hand and playfully flicked it in Brittany's face.

She jumped back and yelled at him, "You jerk! You will so pay for that!" He laughed and went back to washing the rest of the dishes.

"So, what is going on with my file?"

Brittany looked down at the plate she was drying and replied, "You have a sealed file that I can't get access to. I almost always can get into them, but this one says I don't have clearance."

That made Michael curious. *What could be in my past that would be sealed?* "I don't understand. I don't have anything in my past that would be sealed."

"I don't know. Let's finish the dishes and go look at it." They put away the dishes and headed to her spare room.

Michael looked over the room. She had plaques all over the walls. All the things she had accomplished in her life intimidated him because he hadn't been able to go to college. He felt that she was way too smart for him. *Why in the world would a woman like Brittany want to be with me? She's not only beautiful, but smart with goals and a head on her shoulders. I'm a fresh out of jail loser; nothing more and nothing less.*

While Michael was lost in his thoughts, Brittany was booting up her computer. She pulled a screen up on her computer that had Michael's name on in and got his attention. He looked at the screen that displayed all the charges he ever got. Down at the bottom of the page there was a file that said *Sealed*. He took a closer look at the date; 05/29/1995.

"I don't understand. What could I have done at age five to have a sealed record?"

"I don't know Michael, but it has to be big for me not to be able to get into it. I am going to have a friend of mine see if she can get into it on Monday. I just wanted to see if you knew what it could have been."

Michael went over and sat on the couch. A chill ran across his body as he thought; nothing came to mind. He honestly didn't know what it could be, but he did know that whatever it was had to be big. "Okay that's fine. I just don't have any clue what it would be. Maybe my mom will know. I just don't know how the hell I'm going to ask her about it, but I'll figure it out."

Michael sighed and then continued, "Right now, there isn't anything we can do about that file. Let's make the rest of our day together good."

She looked up at him and smiled, "What do you have in mind?" He could think of one thing he would want to do to her, but he wasn't going to push that right now.

"It does involve going out somewhere, but I don't think anyone will notice you where we are going. You don't even have to change. Just let me grab my shirt and stuff and we can go, okay?"

She jumped up and said, "Okay I'm going to put my shoes on I'll meet you outside."

Once dressed and ready to go, Michael met Brittany outside. She was standing next to her car. "Are we taking yours or mine?"

He laughed at how cute and happy she was being. "We can take your car, but I'm driving because this is my treat to you."

She stopped smiling. He hoped she wasn't one of those girls that wouldn't let anyone drive her car. "Okay but can you please give me a hint about where we are going?" *Shew!*

He was glad she wasn't all into her car.

"No hints. It isn't a long drive. Calm down." He got into the car and started the engine then headed out of the driveway and away from town. She normally didn't like surprises much so it was different for her to go along with Michael's plan.

He got into the next town over from theirs and found himself on Main Street; just where he wanted to be. He parked next to the curb. "I'll be right back, just sit tight." She smiled at him and he jumped out of the car and ran down the street. He dipped into a store and back out after getting some things. He crossed the road and went into another store. Once done with that store, he walked back to the car with his bags. He got in the car and placed everything in the back of the car. He started up the car and continued on his journey to the surprise location.

# CHAPTER EIGHT

Brittany was excited to see where Michael was taking her. She was thrilled to be getting away for the day with him. She didn't go out of town much and definitely had never been to that particular small town. She assumed they had stopped in the heart of the little town. It was busy and had a lot of stores in it. The sidewalks were lined up with people laughing and walking by the car. Some stopped almost as if to see who was in the car, but her windows were dark and she knew they couldn't see inside. She tried to see what store Michael went into but she lost him with the crowd of people. It wasn't long and he was back in the car with some bags. She couldn't see what was in the bags but she could smell something familiar. Some type of food and what smelled like flowers, but she couldn't be sure. Michael looked over at her, smiled, and grabbed her hand as he asked, "Are you ready to go?"

Her heart was racing and she didn't know why. "I have no idea where we are going, but yes I'm ready." She smiled back at him and they took off down the busy road.

Once out of the main part of the town, the roads began to twist and turn. She could see mountains above her and minutes later they were half way up the mountain. She yawned so she could get her ears to pop and Michael laughed at her. "Not much further, we are going to the top." She was excited and ready to get there.

They reached the top of the mountain and she was taken

aback by how beautiful it was. She had been in the mountains before but it was different being with Michael. Michael stopped so she could take in the view. She could see the town that they were just in. She could make out houses all down the mountain. It was so peaceful up there and she felt calm; no loud noises, no people, no cars, no phones. It was perfect.

She looked over at Michael. He grabbed her leg and gently squeezed. "I promise we are almost there." He got back on the road and turned off on a small one lane gravel road.

Within a few minutes the car stopped in a meadow. Trees surrounded the meadow except for one area. It looked to be a cliff or a drop off but Brittany wasn't sure. Michael grabbed the bags and jumped out of the car. Once around the car, he opened her door. She got out and took in the view for a few minutes; birds chirping, squirrels and rabbits running around, and even a small fox leaped by. She had never seen a more beautiful place. Brittany walked over to where the tree line stopped and saw it was a cliff. It dropped off the mountain so she stayed a few feet back to be safe.

Once she knew she was in a safe spot, she looked down the drop off. It was amazing. No houses in sight. There were only other mountains around them, some taller and some smaller. Birds flew by everywhere. She was amazed that it was so untouched by people. There were no trails, roads, or parks on the mountains; it was just open to wildlife. She could even see a waterfall on the mountain closest to her. It was amazing and now her favorite place to be. She turned around and found Michael sitting in the middle of the meadow. The bags were gone and the stuff in them was on the ground. She walked over to him to see what he was doing.

She sat next to him on the ground to see what all he had

laying on the ground. There were flowers, an old spy glass, sandwiches, a small portable radio, and a disposable camera. She looked up at him and smiled. "You did all this for me? But why?"

"This used to be my favorite place to be. My mom always took me here when I was little. Not much has changed over the years. I always thought that someone would come and build a house up here but I guess no one ever did. Mom would let me play out here for hours and we would always have food with us or a snack. I brought you here to get away from all of the craziness of the world. There isn't a town out here or people to bother us. It's just nature and the wild. I know you didn't want to be seen in public with me so this was the best idea I had. If you don't like it, we can leave?"

"No. I love it! This is the most beautiful place I have ever been to. Thank you for sharing it with me."

He smiled at her and looked down at the stuff on the ground. "Well these flowers are for you. I hope you like them. I got them to remind you of this place. Every flower that is in this bouquet can be found in this meadow. I got the camera for you as well, so you could take pictures of anything you wanted in the meadow. The food is for us in case you get hungry. It's not much, just peanut butter and jelly, so if you want something else we can stop on the way home. I got the spy glass so you could get a closer look at the other mountains. There are some amazing sights out there that I want to show you. The radio is just to, of course play music. I love music and when in the meadow, it makes it that much more peaceful."

Michael looked at her and waited for her to respond. Brittany almost felt like crying she was so happy. That was the best thing anyone had ever did for her. It took a lot of thinking to put it all together on a short notice and she appreciated it. The more she thought about all of what he did the more she wanted to cry. How could someone so amazing get locked up for such a horrible thing? He spent eight years of his life in prison for something he didn't do. He was too great of a person to be done that way and she knew it. She felt a tear run down her cheek so she looked away from Michael.

"Britt? What's the matter? Did I do something wrong? Was this a bad idea? Please look at me, Britt."

She wiped away the tear and looked at him with a smile. "It's just that I don't get that you would do all this for me. I also don't get why anyone would want to frame you. You are amazing to me and it just hurts to know that someone could be so mean and put you in prison for a crime you didn't commit."

He took his hand and placed it on her face. He kissed her softly and leaned back. "Don't worry about all that right now. Let's just enjoy this for a little bit and then we will deal with the rest later, okay?"

She nodded her head, smiled, grabbed the spy glass, and jumped up heading to the cliff. "So, what should I look for?"

He was right behind her in a flash. "Well, find the waterfall and tell me what you see?" She put the spy glass to her eyes and looked around. She finally found it. There were birds all around the water at the base of the water fall and even had what looked like a mountain lion drinking next to the falls. It was beautiful that it left her speechless.

They spent a while taking turns looking through the spy glass finding different things before Michael grabbed her hand and led her back to the spot on the ground. He picked up the camera and took her picture.

She frowned. "I hate having my picture taken."

He laughed. "Well I guess you won't like the first four I took of you when we got here." She had no idea he took pictures of her when they got there. She was so struck by the place she didn't even pay attention to what Michael was doing.

"Oh, whatever. Let me see that thing."

She grabbed the camera and snapped a picture of him. "So how does that feel, Mr. Sims?"

He jumped up and chased after her. He finally caught her, picked her up, and spun her around off the ground. She laughed and he put her back down. She went to the cliff and looked down at the camera. She had ten more pictures left. She took three of the mountains and decided to save the other seven for another time. They ate their lunch and packed up all their things.

It was around two o'clock when they arrived back at her house. It was by far the best day she had in a long time. She hoped that she and Michael would have more like it. They walked into the house and set the stuff down on the kitchen bar. When Michael turned around and faced her, she knew he was about to leave. She felt a sudden sadness hit her. She didn't want him to go, but she knew he had to. He had a life and so did she. Plus, she needed to call her friend Christine and see if she could get into that file. It might have been Saturday but her friend would do anything for her, plus she owed her a favor. Michael headed for the door and she followed.

She looked down at her hands for a minute and back up to his eyes. "Today was the most amazing day that I have ever had and I owe it all to you. Thank you, Michael. I haven't laughed like that in...well, in forever. I really hope we can visit that place again."

He placed his hands on the sides of her face. "Of course

we can. Thank you for making today amazing Britt. I should get home. My phone is dead and I'm sure my mom is worried sick. I'll call you in a bit, if that's okay?" He kissed her on the lips and pulled away from her and grabbed the door knob.

"Okay. I'll be home all day today. I am going to put a call into my friend and see if she can get that file opened."

He shot her a smile and a nod. In a flash, he was in his truck and driving away from her house. Brittany felt empty with him gone. Closing the door, she walked back into her office and picked up the phone. She dialed Christine's number and waited for her to answer.

*\*\**

Michael drove away from Brittany's house feeling happier than he had in a long time. She made his life so much better then he could have ever hoped for. When he looked back, he saw Brittany's sad face watching him leave. He had no choice but to leave, with a dead phone his mom would not have a way to contact him. Plus, he needed to get home and shower. He drove straight home not stopping anywhere on the way.

Once he got home he saw a cop car sitting outside his mom's house. His smile quickly faded away. *This couldn't be good. Why is a cop at my house?* His heart sank, was his mom okay? He pulled in the driveway and jumped out of the truck racing inside the front door. His mom was seated on the couch with a small cut on her hand. "What happened mom?" He ran over to her side not even looking at the cop sitting in the other chair. He lifted her hand to look at the cut closer. "You have some glass in your hand. Did you break something?"

His mom looked up at Michael and smiled a soft smile. "Michael, I'm fine. Someone threw a rock in our window and when I went to clean up the glass I got a cut on my hand. It was probably just some kid in the neighborhood getting into trouble. Really, I'm fine. The officer was just getting my statement about what happened. I told him to just leave it be, but he won't listen to me."

He looked over at the cop sitting near him. Not just any cop but Officer Johnson. "You came in here worried something was wrong with your mom. Wanna tell me why? It's not how I would have guessed you would react to a cop being at your house. Did you know your mom would be hurt?"

*This son of a bitch. He would be the one to come here.* "My answers don't matter to you. Why are you really here Johnson?" How the hell Brittany could be the daughter of that monster he would never understand.

"Look kid, your mom's window was broken out by a large rock. So here I am just taking my statement. Now that you're here, you can give me one as well."

Michael sat back down next to his mom. "I wasn't here so there isn't anything for me to say. If you have my mother's statement it would be nice if you could leave now." Michael was trying hard for his mom not to freak out on Officer Johnson.

"That's right, your mom said you were gone all night staying at a friend's house. Mind telling me what friend? You know just in case the other cops want to consider some things."

That did it for Michael. He knew the only reason that jackass was there was because he wanted a reason to pin him for something.

"No, I'm not telling you where I was because I don't have to. I am in no way related to what happened here. So, take your nosey ass out of my mother's home!"

His mother jumped up and looked at him. "Michael that's no way to be. Officer, I'm sorry. After what he went through he just doesn't trust the police."

Officer Johnson just shook his head. "Well ma'am, I am going to run. Here is my card and if you think of anything please let me know. As for you Michael, I'll make sure to put down that you don't have an alibi. You know, just for the other cops asking." With that being said, Officer Johnson left.

# CHAPTER NINE

Michael saw red when Officer Johnson was in his mother's house. Why did it matter where he was at? Did he really think Michael would throw a rock in the window of his mother's house? Of course, he would think he did it! Why else would Johnson ask him for an alibi? He needed to call Brittany and let her know about her dad. He wanted her to know he didn't tell him at all about them being together and he wouldn't. First, he had to find out exactly what happened with his mom.

"Mom, I'm sorry I got so upset. I just don't get why the cop that put me away for murder has to be here about a broken window. Please let me look at your hand and get the glass out while you tell me from the beginning what happened today, okay?"

She sat down on the couch while he went and grabbed a first aid kit from under the kitchen sink. He sat next to her and picked out the glass with some tweezers. Then he cleaned it with alcohol wipes and applied an antibiotic ointment. Making a bandage wasn't hard because he made plenty in prison over the years. Once the bandage was applied, he hugged her tight.

"I am glad you're okay. Now tell me step by step what happened."

She looked up at him with a smile on her face. It seemed like no matter what she was always smiling. He loved that about her. The world could be falling around them, she would smile and the problems were gone.

"I was washing dishes and the phone rang. When I answered it no one said anything. I just hung up and went back to the kitchen but before I got there the window above the sink shattered. I was so scared and confused Michael! I didn't know what to do so I called the police. I didn't even get a good look at who did it. Once my nerves calmed down, I realized that it was probably just a kid causing trouble. It had to be nothing."

He could tell she was scared still. "Wait a minute mom. You said you didn't get a good look, but you did at least see someone?"

"Yes, I saw someone tall running through the yard and jump the fence. They weren't in the best of shape because they struggled a little getting over the fence."

Something told Michael that it was the killer. Between the phone call and the window someone was trying to send him a message. He didn't fully understand it but he knew he would get to the bottom of it one way or the other.

Michael got his mom calmed back down and cleaned up what was left of the glass. He found a board out in the back yard and put it over the window until he could get another one put in. Once he got everything done he looked at the stove for the time. It was five forty-five. He went to his room and put his phone on the charger, turned it on, and called Brittany. It didn't take her long to answer.

"Hello?" Her voice did it every time; it made him forget everything.

"Hey Britt, look I called because when I got home your dad was here. Long story short someone threw a rock in my mom's window and scared her pretty bad. They don't know who did it but your dad seemed to zone in on me. He asked where I was and if I had an alibi. I didn't tell him I was with you and don't worry, I won't. They have no reason to look at me for doing something like this. I think your dad was just checking in on me to be honest. Anyway, I just wanted to let you know before word got around." He hated keeping their life a secret and he honestly didn't know how long he could keep going on with that. He was willing to stick with it for then though.

"Wow, I really don't get my dad sometimes. Thank you, for not saying anything. That means a lot. Who do you think threw the rock at your mom's window?"

"I don't know but I think it was the killer. I'm going to talk my mom into staying with a friend of hers for a while just to make sure she is safe."

Brittany's sweet voice got softer "It's crazy to say this, but I miss you Michael."

"I miss you too Britt," he said with a smile bigger than he ever had before. "Look I should go see if I can get my mom to go to her friend's tonight. Is it okay if I call you back in just a little while or do you have something to do?"

"No I don't have anything planned today so just call whenever." He hung up the phone with Brittany and went to find his mom.

*** 

After the mysterious man threw the rock in the window he jumped the fence and ran like a bat out of hell. Then he waited for everything to calm down before he came back to hide out again. He saw Michael pull in the drive way. When Michael and the cop showed up it was a real party then. He couldn't help but smile. *How ironic that the cop that put him in prison is the one that came for the broken window?* The mysterious man laughed in his mind. He sat back closer to the bushes and trees when Michael came into view of the house. He wanted to know where Michael had been throughout the night and majority of all day. Michael might leave again but this time he was ready. He wouldn't leave the tree line until Michael did. His plans were coming together slowly. He couldn't rush it; he had to take his time with all of it. He checked his watch and sat against a tree. He was going to find where Michael was going even if it killed him.

***

Luckily Michael was able to talk his mom into staying with her friend for a few days. She didn't want to at first but knowing that Michael would be gone to work during the days changed her mind. He had the house to himself but he just didn't want to be alone. He wanted to be with Brittany more than anything. He couldn't stop thinking of her. He yearned to be in her presence. He laid on his bed for a little while until his mind had enough. He grabbed some clothes and went to take a shower. Once out of the shower he grabbed his overnight bag and packed it full of things he might need. Keys in hand, he went to his truck.

He pulled up to Brittany's house now wondering if it was a good idea. Either way it was too late to change his mind. He left his bag in the car and figured he would see her reaction before he took it inside. He knocked on the door and waited for her to answer. It took her a while but soon he heard footsteps coming toward the door. She opened the door with a shocked expression on her face. Her face changed and she was smiling really big. It didn't take her long to jump up and hug him.

"Wait, why are you here? Is something wrong?"

He pulled back from her so he could look at her a little better. She had a bright blue tank top on and some fitted blue jeans. She looked sexy as hell and he didn't know how long he could stand it. The tank top made her already big breast look even bigger, and the jeans fit her ass like her own skin.

"No nothing is wrong. You said you missed me and I missed you. So here I am. Can I come in?"

She grabbed his hand, pulled him inside, and shut the door, so he took that as a yes.

"So, did your mom agree to stay with someone?"

"Yes she did. She is going to stay with her friend for a little while."

She let his hand go and walked down the hall towards the living room area, he followed her. They sat on the couch looking at each other.

"I called my friend about your file. Apparently she doesn't have clearance for it either, but she knows someone who does. It might take a little time but I really think it's worth it. Something keeps nagging at me about that file, you know?"

Oh yeah, he knew because it was eating him alive too. "Yeah, you're right Britt. There is definitely something there. I just don't know what. I didn't even have a chance to ask my mom what it could be. If nothing comes back from your friend, I'll ask her about it. She is just shook up right now and I'm not so sure it would be good to bring up more problems right now."

She scooted over closer to him on the couch. He looked at Brittany. "We do need to talk about something Britt."

She looked up at him with her big blue eyes. "Okay, what's up?" He hated to bring her mood down but it wasn't something he could keep putting off.

"What are we going to do about us? I mean do you always want me to be hidden behind a closed door? That will get old after a while. I know you are worried about your dad being upset and I get that. I guess what I'm trying to say is...Will I always have to hide us from the world?" She looked away from him and he could see the hurt in her eyes. He knew the answer before she even spoke.

"For now, that's just how it has to be. Once we clear your name, then we can work our way into public. I'm just not ready to tell anyone yet. I can't expect you to wait around for that to happen, so I understand if you don't want to."

She looked back at him waiting for an answer and to be honest he didn't have one yet. He hadn't thought about it a lot and he knew he wouldn't like being in the dark the whole time. Questions ran through his mind over and over. *What if we don't find the killer? What if her dad still hates me even after we find the killer? What if she is ashamed to be with him?* He knew he had to let the what ifs go and deal with everything right then.

"I'll wait Britt. We will find the killer and go from there." She smiled and they started talking about family and getting to know each other more.

***

The mysterious man followed Michael to a drive way on the outskirts of town. He parked his car down the road a bit and got out. Running through the trees he came to a house in the woods, and spotted Michael's truck. Michael was on the porch talking to someone. He got as close as he could without being seen. He could hear a little bit of their conversation. Something about missing him so there he was. From what he could hear it sounded like he was talking to someone he really liked, but who?

He had to get closer and see who it was before they went inside. He went around the back of the house and cut across to the trees in the front yard; keeping a good distance between him and the house. Now he could see Michael, but Michael was blocking his view of the girl. Just then Michael moved a little to the side and her face came into view. *Wow! He is sleeping with THE lawyer. Oh man this is good. The idiot is fooling around with the cop's daughter.*

He almost laughed out loud, until he remembered they might hear him. The wheels began to turn in his head and his twisted little mind devised a new plan. *How great would it be to see a story headlined on the news saying: Murderer set free after killing girlfriend eight years ago. Now kills another girlfriend.* He loved his new plan so much. He needed to go back to his hotel and think it all through. He waited for Michael to go inside, and then made his way back to his car. *The cop definitely wouldn't make a deal with that little shit if he thought he killed his daughter.*

# CHAPTER TEN

Brittany thought about the fact that someone had broken Michael mother's window earlier that day. She was even more surprised that her dad responded to the call. He wasn't the type of cop to respond to small petty calls like that. It had to be only because it was Michael's mother. Sometimes Brittany would get so mad at the things her dad did. His gut was usually never wrong, but in Michael's case Brittany knew it was. It also blew her mind that her dad would even ask Michael for an alibi. It didn't make sense. Why in the world would Michael throw a rock into his mother's window? Her dad had to want to just check in on Michael and saw it as the perfect time to.

She was so thankful that Michael didn't say he was with her the night before and all that day. She knew her dad and Michael would have gotten into a fight right then and there. She could feel Michael getting irritated with the fact they couldn't let anyone know about them, but she just couldn't let it get out that she was seeing a "murderer". She was still a lawyer and her dad was still the cop that put Michael away. She knew he wouldn't hide in the dark forever though. She hoped the real killer would be caught; then Michael would be able to live a normal life and they could be a normal couple. Until then, she just couldn't and wouldn't let their relationship get out to the public.

\*\*\*

Michael's arm was asleep from Brittany's head laying on it. They had talked for a little while before Brittany snuggled up to him and fell asleep. He had been playing with her hair when he heard deep breathing coming from Brittany. He knew she was asleep. Not wanting to wake her, he just bit his tongue and let the numbness in his arm take over. Michael's stomach grumbled a little. He hadn't eaten since their lunch date, and it was getting late. Just as his stomach grumbled a little louder Brittany woke up.

She looked up at him smiling. "Your stomach sounds like a monster is living in there." She laughed a little and sat up off his arm.

"Yeah, I'm a little hungry. I haven't eaten since our lunch date today."

"Well it is nine-fifteen. I haven't eaten either; I think a monster is living in me too with the way I feel. I don't have anything in here to eat though."

"Well do you want to order some pizza? I mean if people deliver to your house. You do live kind of out in the middle of nowhere," he said as he tried to hide his smile.

"Yes, people deliver out here, sir! I'm going to go order the pizza. I like supreme, is that okay?" He shook his head and sat back on the couch.

Once she walked back into the kitchen he tried to think of a way to be able to stay at her house tonight.

Brittany walked back into the living room a few minutes later with two beers. *Man, she knows the way to a man's heart.* She sat next to him on the couch and handed him one of the beers. He took the beer and gave her a kiss on the forehead.

Brittany curled up next to him and sighed. "Do you have anything to do tonight?"

He knew he didn't have anything more important than being here with her. "Nope. Just hanging out with you until you kick me out." He smiled at her and took another sip of his beer.

"I don't want to kick you out Michael. I was about to ask if you wanted to stay? I seem to sleep better with you here and I would love your company...I mean if you want to stay."

She took a swig of her beer and looked at him waiting for him to answer. Well, that solved his problem because he didn't need to ask if he could stay; she already did it for him.

"I would love to stay. As a matter of fact, I packed a bag hoping you would let me stay."

She laughed. "Well go get it, dummy, and make yourself at home. I'm going to run up and change. The pizza will be here in about thirty minutes by the way."

She jumped up off the couch and ran off to her room. Michael put his beer down and went out to the truck to get his bag. Once he came back in with his bag he raced up stairs to Brittany's room to change. The door to her room was open so he just went in. It quickly became apparent that he should have knocked because Brittany was standing at her closet door completely naked.

He couldn't turn his eyes away from her, even though he felt like he should. She reached up in the top of the closet to grab a tank top. Her long legs shining in the moon light from the window. Her hair fell down her back almost touching the top of her butt. Her body was perfect. She had curves that were amazing. Her breasts were full and had just the right amount of perkiness to let you know they were real. He could see a hint of a few scars across her belly. He wondered where they were from. He looked away before she could catch him staring.

"I'm sorry. I should have knocked. I came up to change. I'll go change in the bathroom."

He walked by her without looking, to give her some privacy. Once in the bathroom, he changed into some basketball shorts and put away his shirt he wore that day and his pants. He stepped out of the bathroom to find Brittany standing in front of him with a tank top and boy shorts on. Just when he thought she couldn't get sexier, she did. He smiled from ear to ear.

"You have no idea how beautiful you are, do you? Not just on the outside Britt, on the inside too."

He grabbed her hand with his empty hand and pulled her close to him. He kissed her gently and ran his fingers up and down her arm. She got cold chills instantly.

"We should head down stairs. The pizza will be here soon."

She looked in his eyes and said, "Yeah, I'm pretty hungry. You can put your bag on the bed if you want. Oh, and thank you for the compliment. That means a lot. I haven't felt pretty in a long time, and you're starting to make me feel that way again. So, thank you."

He placed his bag on the bed and followed her back downstairs to the living room. She grabbed the remote and turned on the TV. They found a funny Kevin Hart movie and decided to wait until the pizza got there to start it. The doorbell rang and Michael jumped up as Brittany did.

"I'll get it babe just go sit down and relax." She rolled her eyes but went back to the living room. She yelled out at him as he walked away.

"It's already paid for. Oh, and the tip is too!"

He had a feeling she would do that. It didn't make him

mad. He knew Brittany was the type of girl who didn't want a guy to buy everything for her. She just needed to get used to a guy buying ALMOST everything for her. He reached the door and looked out the peephole before he opened it. He grabbed the pizza and gave the guy a few extra dollars; he wanted to contribute at least a little to their dinner. He placed the pizza on the counter and got two plates out of the cabinets. Once back in the living room with their plates he handed her one. They ate their pizza and watched the movie. Once the movie ended, Brittany yawned really big.

Michael knew she was tired. "You ready to head to bed? You look tired and I'm getting there too."

She nodded her head yes.

"Oh, don't worry about the mess, I'll get it in the morning."

Once in Brittany's room Michael put his bag in the floor by the bed and slid off his shorts. He grabbed his toothbrush and toothpaste out of the bag, and headed to the bathroom. Brittany followed behind him. They both stood at the double sink brushing their teeth, every so often catching a glance at each other smiling. They finished brushing their teeth and headed to bed.

Michael scooted closer to Brittany in the bed. He laid on his side to get a better view of her face. She turned on her side just as he did, and he placed his hand on her face and ran his fingers through her hair. Her eyes closed and she sighed. She opened her eyes and stared into his. For a moment time seemed to stand still.

"If you want to go to sleep Britt I'll let you go to sleep. Before you decide if you want to or not, you should know that if you say no I won't be able to stop myself anymore."

He knew that Brittany knew what he meant. He had been

able to control himself so many other times with her, but he knew if he kissed her then he wouldn't be able to stop at just that. His heart was pounding out of his chest as he awaited her response.

*** 

Brittany heard what Michael said to her but it just didn't register in her brain. She wanted him badly and knew she wouldn't stop him. Her heart was pounding so hard she could feel it in her head thumping.

"I'm not tired right now Michael and I won't stop you."

He took his hand, the one he ran through her hair, and placed it at the base of her neck. He pulled her hair gently and forced her face closer to his.

"I have been doing my best to not make any moves on you that you don't want babe. Just know that I have wanted to do this for a very long time."

He slowly placed his body on top of hers, gently resting her legs on the outside of his. He bent down closer to her face. With forcefulness, he kissed her hard. She moaned in his mouth and kissed him with a sense of urgency. She felt his body rubbing against hers. She could feel how hard he was getting from kissing her. He wanted her, but she wanted him more. He stopped kissing her and moved his hands to her shirt, pulling the straps on her tank top down. A fear ran through her mind. She didn't want him to see her stomach. She lost a lot of weight over the years, but scars still showed where weight had once been.

He tried to pull her shirt off but she stopped him. "That's the one thing I will stop you from. You can pull it down, just not off. I don't want my stomach showing."

He looked confused for a second but didn't push the issue. He pulled her top down and her breast flung out. With both hands, he grabbed each breast and squeezed a little. He leaned down and began to bite and suck one of her nipples. She arched her back and moaned loudly. She never felt like her body belonged to anyone before, but now she knew it was Michael's and always would be. She was lost for so long and she needed him. He placed kisses up her chest, to her neck, and back down to her breast. He sat up and looked up at her. His eyes were dark with a hunger in them like she had never seen before.

His hands ran down her sides to her waist. Placing his fingers in the rims of her panties, he began to pull them down her legs. He shifted her legs and pulled them off, throwing them onto the floor. Her breath was shorter and louder. She watched every move Michael made. He kissed her ankle trailing kisses the rest of the way up her leg to her waist then back down the other leg to the other ankle. She arched her back moaning, unsure if it tickled or if it was pleasure taking over. Her body was boiling and she was throbbing. He trailed kisses back up her leg as she squirmed all over the place. She was so wet and hot that she couldn't take much more. It had been so long since her body was touched and she couldn't take it. "Please," she moaned. He looked up at her not taking his eye off her as he slipped a finger inside her. She bit her lip, moaning, trying not to look away from him. Sliding his finger faster, she wanted to find her release, she needed it. Her body shivered and she knew it was close.

"Don't stop it, baby," he whispered to her.

She let go, bucking her back up, she grabbed the sheets hard as her body jolted in pleasure. He removed his finger and got off the bed. She looked up and saw him taking off his boxers. He climbed back on top of her, positioning her legs around his body. He locked eyes with her and entered her. She felt pain and pleasure all at once.

She closed her eyes trying to save this moment. "Open your eyes Britt; I want you to keep your eyes open for me." She opened her eyes.

He leaned down and kissed her face as he started to move slowly. She moaned in his mouth as her body matched his movements. He bit her ear as he gained speed and went deeper. She was about to let go again and he knew it.

"Britt, cum with me baby. Let go with me."

They both lost control at the same time, moaning together. He kissed her softly, slowly pulling out of her. He pulled away and laid next to her; quickly pulling her close to him. They both were out of breath. Neither of them said a word for a while. Eventually Michael spoke first.

"Baby that was more then I could have ever thought it would be."

She knew exactly what he was trying to say. Their bodies fit perfect together, like they were made for each other.

"I never thought I would say this but...that was magical in so many ways."

They laid there not speaking again that night. Words couldn't describe what they felt, but they both knew it was only one thing...love. They eventually drifted off to sleep.

# CHAPTER ELEVEN

I t had been almost week since Brittany and Michael spent the night together. Brittany told Taylor everything when she confronted her about Michael calling the office trying to find her; of course, leaving out big details. She thought Taylor would have a stroke when she told her about Michael but amazingly she didn't. Taylor was happy for her and promised not to tell anyone. However, she didn't promise to not pick on Brittany about it. Somehow Taylor managed to bring up Michael every day. It never really mattered anyway because Brittany was always thinking of Michael.

She and Michael hadn't gone one day without talking on the phone that week. She hadn't seen him since he left Sunday afternoon. They'd spent the day lying around watching movies. Saturday night still ran through her mind very often. She knew she should back off but she couldn't. She was in love with Michael and she knew it, but there was no way she would tell him that yet though. She liked things the way they were and she wanted to keep it that way as long as she could.

It was Friday and Brittany was busier than ever. She looked at the wall where her clock was at. It was six thirty. It was getting late but she wanted to get more done before leaving. She paged Taylor to come to her office for a second. Five minutes later Taylor walked in her office.

Brittany looked up at her. "I need to get some more stuff done but it's already six thirty. I'm going to take some work home and finish what I can over the weekend. Can you do me a favor?"

Taylor shot her a sneaky grin. "You won't be able to work if lover boy is at your house. Either way what do you need me to do?"

Even though her comment irritated Brittany, she knew Taylor was right.

"Can you go over my report on Mrs. Lane before you mail it off? I know it's late so if you want to do it over the weekend that's fine."

Taylor nodded and started for the door. Before she left she turned to face Brittany again.

"Are you heading out now? I am going to take the report home and if you want I'll walk out with you just let me grab my bag."

"Yeah, I just have to grab a few things and I'll meet you at the front office."

Taylor left and Brittany scooped up some more papers and her laptop and placed them in her briefcase. She met Taylor at the front office.

"So, any big plans this weekend Taylor?"

She smiled at Taylor and headed for the front door.

"No not much at all. Me and the hubby are going to dinner tomorrow night but that's about it. What about you?"

"Not much just work and hanging out with Michael probably."

They had plans to go to the next town over again but this time they were going to get groceries so they could cook over the weekend. She was just excited to spend time with him outside the house. Taylor smiled and opened the door for Brittany. She stopped and didn't walk out the door almost like she forgot something.

"Oh shit, Britt. I forgot you got a package today! Hang on it's in my desk drawer. Let me go grab it."

Brittany was confused. *Who sent me a package? Maybe Michael did. No, why would he send me something when we planned on meeting in an hour at my house? That didn't make sense. Oh well, whatever it is, I'll open it later.*

Taylor came running to the door with a small package. She handed it to Brittany and they made their way to each other's cars.

"If you need anything on the report, just let me know. I might need to get with you this weekend to go over some more papers if you're free. I'll buy some pizza or Chinese if you want?"

"That sounds good. Just let me know what day and I'll be there. See you later, Britt."

Taylor got in her car and was gone in a flash. Brittany sat in her car with it running for a minute. She looked for a return address on the package but there wasn't one. *Well that's weird.* She tossed it in the seat next to her and drove home. When Brittany got home, she placed her stuff down on the counter in the kitchen and ran upstairs to change.

Brittany changed into a pair of shorts and a plain gray shirt and thought about Michael's file. Her friend Christine still hadn't called her about the sealed file. Brittany knew it would take a little while but she was becoming impatient. *I need to give her a call.* If she and Christine didn't have access to the file, there was a good chance a lot of people didn't. Michael tried to talk to his mom about it but she refused to talk about any of it. He left it alone and said he would try to talk to her again in a few more days. Whatever it was Brittany felt would help solve who the killer was.

She ran back downstairs to the kitchen and grabbed all her work items. She left the package on the counter and headed to her office. Michael would be there soon so she wanted to get her stuff put away before he came. Brittany got distracted by some of her papers she brought home and lost track of time. She heard a knock on the door and figured it was Michael. She walked to the door and looked out the peephole. Sure enough. It was him. She opened the door and let him in.

She reached up and kissed him on the cheek and he hugged her.

"Hey. How was work?"

"It was really long, but it was okay,.."

They walked hand in hand to the kitchen.

"Get something in the mail today?"

"Yeah, it came at work and Taylor forgot to give it to me until we were about to leave."

She walked by him, pulled out a pair of scissors from a drawer, and cut open the package. She looked inside and was suddenly really confused. It was a book and a piece of paper. She shook the book and paper on the counter and reached to grab it. Before she could touch it, Michael grabbed her hand and jerked it back.

"Don't touch that Britt!"

She looked at him like he was crazy. It was sent to her not him, so why did he look like it was his?

"Why can't I touch it?"

"Britt that is the diary that I told you was missing from Ashley's room."

*Oh, my God!* Who would send this to her? Why would they send it to her? Brittany was shocked and could feel her head spinning. She felt like she was going to pass out so she reached for the island to settle herself. Michael wrapped his arms around her.

"Are you okay, Britt? Come on let's get you to the living room."

He helped her walk to the living room and she sat down on the couch. She was breathing fast and her heart was going crazy.

"Michael, who sent me that and why?"

"I don't know why they sent it to you Britt but I know it had to be the killer. Do you have any gloves?"

She was lost in her own mind then. *The killer sent this to me? Why? Is he coming for me now? This just doesn't make any sense.*

"Yes, in the top drawer of the kitchen island."

He left her and ran to the island. She was scared, worried, and beyond angry. If someone wanted to scare her then they did a good job of it. She was freaking out and had no clue what to do.

\*\*\*

Michael found the gloves in the drawer. They were a little too small for his hands but he didn't care. That son of a bitch sent the diary to Brittany and he had no clue why. If anyone tried to hurt Brittany, he would kill them. He reached down and carefully opened the folded paper. Written in red ink was, "Plans changed. Ashley. Brittany." *This mother fucker is after Brittany now!* Michael saw red and almost blacked out from anger. It was obvious that whoever it was just wanted to hurt anyone close to Michael. He knew what he had to do, but he knew Brittany wouldn't like it one bit. He reached down and picked up Ashley's diary and skimmed through the old worn pages. He felt wrong for reading any of it but he had to see what the last few pages said. Maybe it would give him some kind of clue to what was going on. He found the last entry. It was the day Ashley was murdered. It read:

Diary,

Today Michael and I are going out with some friends. I don't really care where we go as long as I'm with him I'm ok. I keep feeling like someone has been following me the past few days. It's probably nothing but today I just have a bad feeling. There was an older man parked on the side of the road a few miles from my house. He stared at me as I drove past him. He looked weird and I'm not sure how to describe it. I guess maybe I'm just letting things get to my head. Either way I am going to forget everything and go out tonight and have some fun.

Love always,

Ashley

Who was the man she saw that day? This had Michael thinking really hard. He didn't remember seeing any cars on the side of the road when he went to see Ashley. It had to be the killer though. Maybe it was on a different road, she could have taken the back way to her house. He turned the page, figuring it would be blank, but it wasn't. In red ink, there was a message addressed to Michael.

*You know too much Michael. Love will fall and you will be blamed. This is your fault and her blood will be on your hands. Just like Ashley's. I'M COMING SOON!*

Michael closed the diary and placed it all back into the

package. He tried not to lose his shit in front of Brittany, but he was so damn mad. If he got the chance to come face to face with the killer Michael was going to make sure he died a slow painful death. He didn't care if someone threatened him, but threatening someone he loved and cared about was a different story. He didn't take the killer seriously when he wrote down his mother's name. This time it was different. The killer was trying to prove just how serious he really was. Michael didn't like it at all.

Michael went back to the living room carrying a glass of wine in his hand. He sat down next to Brittany. He handed her the wine and she whispered thank you to him. He wouldn't let anything happen to her even if that meant his life would end. He wasn't going to let Brittany out of his sight as much as possible.

"Drink that and try to relax for a little bit, okay? Do you have a safe?"

She looked at him confused.

"Yes, there is one in my office and one under my bed. Why?"

He grabbed her hand and kissed it.

"I need to put that stuff in your safe while we are gone. We are going to go out to the store and act as normal as we can. We will talk about this more while we are out, okay?"

She just nodded, stood up and started to walk out of the living room. He got up and followed her. He stopped in the kitchen and grabbed the package.

"Let's put it in the one under your bed okay?"

She tried to force a smile at him but he could tell she was scared. That was the part about all this that made him even angrier. He hated seeing her scared and worried. It was like she was hurting and he was lost with what to do to comfort her.

"That's fine. Come on I'll show you the combination."

After placing the package in the safe he pushed it back under the bed. He stood up and faced Brittany. Touching her arm, he pulled her in a hug to comfort her.

"Britt, I promise that I won't let anything happen to you. This is all my fault. If I would have just stayed away and never kissed you then you wouldn't be wrapped up in this shit. I don't regret kissing you though. I would be lost without you. I never thought I would be able to find someone. I definitely never thought I would fall in love with someone as amazing as you. I am the luckiest guy in the world to even have a chance with you Britt. Please trust me when I say I'll protect you, baby."

She pulled back and kissed him hard on the lips.

"I know you will Michael. I am scared and really worried but please know that when you're here I feel safe. And, I feel the same way about you. I never thought I would ever have another chance at love. I gave up and dedicated my life to working. Then you came along and here I am getting that chance. It's crazy to say this but even with all this madness going on, I am the happiest I have ever been. Please don't blame yourself for any of this. It isn't your fault that someone is out there acting crazy. We will figure this out together step by step."

He smiled at her. She amazed him more and more with every day. She was full of surprises and knew right then that no matter what he was going to make sure Brittany was his forever.

"Let's go to the store and get us some food for the weekend. I don't know what our next move is with the diary but I do know you aren't getting rid of me this weekend. Lucky you, right?"

He laughed and then kissed her on the forehead.

"Well I didn't plan on you leaving at all this weekend either so let's go to the store and plan out our weekend. Oh, and don't let me forget ice cream! We are making sundaes tonight."

He couldn't stop smiling. He was happy he could make her forget what was going on even for a second and damn it if ice cream would help with that then he was going to buy as much as he could for her. They got in the car and started out the driveway. Michael planned to use that time to map out their plan for the diary. The next town wasn't too far away but it still gave them enough time to figure things out.

# CHAPTER TWELVE

"Britt I think we need to go to the police about the package."

Michael knew she wouldn't go for it at all but he really didn't know what else to do.

"Michael I am not going to the police. In case you didn't know it, my dad is a cop. He would flip out if he knew about me and you. I'm just not ready for that yet."

At that point it didn't matter what she was ready for, he was worried about a killer trying to murder her. He tried not to let her words upset him but it got to him big time. He understood how people would look at her for being with him but was Brittany really the type of person who cared what people think? She had to be for her to act like he was a curse to be in public with. He was hurt at the thought of it.

"Look I understand how bad it would make you look being with me. But what do you want to do about it? Let's be honest, what is worse, being seen with me or having a killer try to kill you? Look Britt, this isn't about your reputation, it's about your life. The note said he was coming for you. I don't want to lose you and I'm not trying to scare you right now but damn Britt this isn't a simple little thing we just push aside."

He regretted his words the minute the words rolled out of his mouth. Brittany didn't say a word and he knew he hurt her.

"Britt, I'm sorry for that. I'm just upset and I honestly don't know what else to do. I know how hard it would be to tell your dad about us. I'm just worried about you and I can't be out in public to protect you. I can keep you safe on the weekend but what about the week days, Britt? Look, if you don't want to tell the cops what's going on then what should we do? Let's talk this out and go from there. If we can't come up with a better option, then we will go back to my idea, okay?"

He waited for her to answer.

"I have a ton of vacation time saved up; I could work from home if I need to. The only problem with that is your job. You just started your job and you can't risk losing it. It's not easy to get a job with a record. My idea was stupid, forget I said anything okay?"

He could tell she was frustrated. Maybe she was onto something though. He knew a job would be hard to find again but he knew it wouldn't be impossible.

"Britt that plan might work. How much time off do you have saved up?"

She looked at him confused for a second.

"Almost three weeks, but then again I am the boss so as long as I need. It won't work though Michael, what about your job?"

They were in the town by then. Michael turned down the

road were the local store was.

"Let me worry about my job Britt. Just put in for your time off and work from home. Do you mind if I stay with you while you're on your time off?"

She looked out the window. He could tell she was still hurt by his earlier rant.

"Britt, look I am really sorry okay?"

She continued to look out of the window. Michael pulled into the store and parked the car.

"Britt look at me please. I'm sorry about what I said. I shouldn't have said it. I was freaking out and taking it out on you and that was wrong of me. I love you Brittany and I don't want to lose you. This is all my fault and if I were to lose you because of some crazy person trying to hurt me, I don't know what I would do. When I got out of prison, my only thought was to find who killed Ashley and get my name cleared. Now I have a reason to live. I don't spend every day planning my revenge on the world for what happened to me, I spend it thinking of how I can better myself for you. I spend it thinking of how I can make you happy. You are my world, Britt. Please understand how sorry I am."

"You love me?" she asked with tears were in her eyes.

"Is that all you caught out of that whole spill I just did?" he asked as he chuckled a little. "Yes, Britt I love you. I pretty much told you that already."

A tear rolled down her cheek and he wiped it away.

"I love you too Michael."

He smiled and kissed her. They got out of the car and went in the store. Michael held her close to him. He could not be public in their town where they knew people but in that town, she was his.

\*\*\*

Once back at Brittany's house, she and Michael put away all the groceries. When they were done, Brittany thought of the fact that she needed to call Taylor to inform her that she was taking some time off. She also planned to see if Taylor could come over that next day so she could explain everything to her in person.

"Michael, I'm going into my office to call Taylor. Just make yourself at home, I shouldn't be too long."

It wasn't late so Brittany figured Taylor and her husband hadn't gone out to eat yet. She walked to her office and closed the door behind her. She picked up the phone and dialed Taylor's number. Taylor answered on the third ring.

"Hey Britt, what's up?"

"What are you doing tomorrow around lunch time?"

"I'm not busy until around four tomorrow. Do you need some help with something?"

"Yeah I need to go over some stuff and I'm also going to be taking some time off for a bit."

"What? Why are you taking time off? Things are crazy right now!"

"I'll explain everything tomorrow, Taylor. I really don't

want to explain it over the phone."

"Blake made plans with his friends. So I'm coming over tonight to find out what's going on whether you like it or not!"

*Well then.* "Okay Taylor I'll see you in a little bit then."

Brittany hung up the phone and went back to the kitchen. Michael was not there so she checked the living room but he wasn't in there either. She ran upstairs to her room and still didn't see him. Then she heard water running in the bathroom. Just as she was about to turn around and run back downstairs, Michael opened the bathroom door.

"Hey, I was about to come down and get you. Did you get a hold of Taylor?"

"Yes, I did and she is coming over tonight. She wants to know what's going on. I have to tell her why I'm taking time off or she will never leave me alone."

"When will she be here?"

"I don't know she said tonight so I probably have about an hour or so. Why?"

He took her hand and led her to the bathroom. When she walked in she was shocked at what she saw. The lights to the bathroom were off and there were candles all over the bathroom floor and around the tub. Michael had run her a bath with a bath bomb in the water, laid out her robe and comfy clothes, and had a glass of wine sitting on the counter. She was speechless.

"I wanted to do something for you so that you could

relax. Is it not okay? You look like you're not happy with it."

Her heart melted and tears ran down her face. She was shocked, but it was amazing. No one had ever done anything like that for her before. How did she get so lucky to find someone like Michael?

"No this is perfect. It's just that no one has ever done anything like this for me before. I love it! Every bit of it is perfect. Thank you, Michael."

She ran her fingers over the water. It was steaming hot, just the way she liked it.

"You're welcome, babe. I am going to let you relax for a little while. I need to make a few calls. I'll come back and check in on you in a bit, okay? Do you need anything else?"

"A kiss," she said with a giggle.

He bent down and kissed her before he moved to the door. Once the door shut, Brittany took her clothes off, grabbed her wine, and sank down into the steaming hot water. Her skin was on fire for a second but soon it became a comfort to her.

\*\*\*

Michael ran down the stairs with a smile on his face. He was so glad that Brittany enjoyed her little surprise he did for her. He wanted to make it up to her for what he said earlier. He hoped it was at least a step in the right direction. He went into the living room to make his phone calls. He wanted to call Mark and let him know what all was going on. He also needed to call and check in on his mom. She was probably playing cards but he still wanted to let her know he wasn't home.

Michael called Mark first. Mark did not answer the phone so he hung up and was about to call his mom when there was a knock on the door. He figured it was Taylor. *I guess Taylor didn't want to wait too long to come by.* He got up and checked to see who it was. Sure enough, it was Taylor. He opened the door and let her in.

"Hey Taylor. Brittany is taking a bath, but come on in."

She smiled at him and went past him to the hall.

"If you want to wait in the living room I'll run up and let her know your here?"

She stood there staring at him like he was a piece of meat.

"That's fine just let her know to take her time."

She walked off to the living room and Michael went upstairs.

Michael tapped on the door before walking in the bathroom.

"Britt, your friend just got here. I sent her to the living room. She said for you to take your time."

He looked over to where she was and could not help but notice how beautiful she was in the candle light. Her hair was wet and steam was rolling off the water. She took a sip of her wine and looked at him.

"Okay, I'll be done soon. Can you grab her a glass of wine? I'm sure she is going to need it."

"I sure can, beautiful."

He went back downstairs and got a glass of wine for Taylor. Once in the living room he spotted Taylor in the recliner by the far wall playing on her phone. He handed her the wine and sat on the couch.

"Britt said she would be down in a second."

He felt a little awkward being in a room alone with Taylor seeing as he didn't really know her. She took a small sip of wine and looked over at him.

"So, I am assuming you know why Brittany is taking time off?"

"Yes, I do, but you should probably hear from her why first."

They sat in silence for a while until Brittany walked in.

"Hey Taylor. Thanks for coming by, but you know you could have come tomorrow."

Brittany laughed a little and sat down by Michael on the couch.

"Yeah, I could have, but me and Blake are fighting so he is out with his friends. Being home wasn't working so here I am. So, tell me what's going on and don't leave anything out!"

Michael and Brittany worked together telling her everything that was going on. From the day Michael went to Brittany about finding the real killer to getting the package. Taylor never said a word the whole time they talked. She waited until they finished before she finally said anything.

"Let me see if I understand you all the way. Michael wanted your help in finding the real killer. You said yes and tried to help in any way you could. Then you found out the killer might be coming for Michael's mom but wasn't for sure. Then you didn't hear anything from the killer since the last note and all a sudden he sends Brittany a package. In the package was the diary of the dead girl Michael went to prison for supposedly killing. It also had a note in it saying he was coming to kill Brittany. In the meantime, you both found a sealed file from Michael's past that you nor Christine have been able to get access to; a file that Michael had no clue existed. Then you decide to take time off work so Michael can protect you. You won't call the police because if your dad finds out you're with Michael he would flip out. On top of that no one, except me, knows that y'all are a thing. Am I getting all of this right?"

"Yeah, that sums it all up."

Taylor whistled and looked at her wine glass.

"I need a refill. I'll be back."

Taylor walked to the kitchen and was back in a few minutes. She sat back down and didn't speak for a while.

"Okay so what is y'all next move? I mean you can't sit around waiting for the psycho to attack. Plus, what if he waits until you go back to work, Brittany? You can't work from home forever."

Michael had already been thinking the same thing in his head.

"Taylor, we are hoping he will make his move before she goes back to work. If not, then we will deal with it all from there. I have a feeling he won't wait that long. Since the police is out, we don't have many other options to go on right now. We are using what we have for the moment."

Taylor looked at Brittany and back to Michael.

"You better take care of her Michael. Cause, if anything happens to her you best believe it won't be just her dad you will deal with. It will be me too."

Michael totally understood Taylor's concern, but he wasn't going to let anyone come near Brittany. Michael looked over to Brittany.

"Do you mind if I use your office to make my phone calls? I was going to do them earlier but Taylor showed up and I didn't want to be rude to your friend."

She nodded and he left the room. He called Mark again hoping to get an answer; which he did.

"Hey dude, I was beginning to think you ran off! What's up?"

"I'm dealing with some shit right now and I haven't been able to bring your key back. Are you busy tomorrow?"

"Not until tomorrow night. Why what's up? You alright man?"

Michael sighed and said, "Can you come over to Brittany's house. I need to talk to you in person and I want to give your key back to you."

"Yeah, I can. What time and where is it?"

"Around lunch time and it's out near the old Mill's farm. Just call me when you're close and I'll tell you how to get here."

They hung up and Michael dialed his mother. She answered him with a lot of noise in the background.

"Now Michael, you know I play cards tonight. Everything okay, honey?"

"Yeah mom I'm fine. I was just calling to check on you and let you know I'm not going to be home for a few days. I'm helping Mark with some stuff so I'm staying with him."

He hated lying to his mom, but he didn't have a choice. His mom ended the phone call saying she was fine and she would call him the next day. Michael got up and went back to the living room to see how Brittany and Taylor were doing.

# CHAPTER THIRTEEN

Brittany watched Michael as he walked out of the living room and headed towards the office. Taylor was staring at her waiting for him to leave.

"Okay Britt, I know I told you to keep him as a side dish but I didn't think all these issues came with it. Are you sure that this is all worth it? I mean with your dad, this crazy guy sending you stuff, on top of Michael and his record. I just want to make sure you have really thought about all this."

Brittany got where Taylor was coming from. She had put a lot more thought in it then Taylor knew.

"It's worth it Taylor. I can't explain it all right now but even in all the madness I have never been happier. I can deal with whatever comes. I know the risk but I'm okay because what I'm getting out of it in the end is worth it. I can deal with my dad later. He might be upset but what can he do? He will love me no matter what. It might take time for him to get over it but I deserve to be happy. As for the crazy guy sending me stuff, I'm safe with Michael, trust me. Besides, the crazy guy just proves that Michael never murdered anyone. I know my dad or anyone else won't see it that way until we have more evidence to prove it, but I know it will all work itself out one way or the other. I promise I have thought about it all Taylor, and this is what I want."

Brittany could see the worry in her Taylor's eyes, but she wanted to change the subject to Taylor and Blake.

"So, tell me what you and Blake were fighting about."

Taylor's mood changed dramatically. Brittany knew it couldn't be good.

"We have been fighting for a long time. We just don't see eye to eye anymore. He asked me for a divorce a few days ago, and I don't know what to do. I love him with all my heart but we've tried everything from counseling to meditation and nothing is working. He is so done with me that it doesn't seem like there is anything I can do to change his mind about us."

Brittany was shocked. Taylor and Blake always seemed so happy, but then again, the last time she had seen them together was about six months prior.

"So, you want to try to work it out, but he doesn't?"

Taylor looked like she wanted to cry but couldn't.

"I honestly don't know anymore. I have tried for about four months to work on it and he's been going through the motions. Of course, he went to counseling and all that but you could tell he just wasn't trying. Even the therapist said Blake was done and just didn't care anymore. He said some people are like light switches once they are off they don't come back on. Blake was done with our marriage and wasn't going to try no matter what. So, about a month ago, I got to the point where I felt like if he wasn't going to try then neither was I. So, in a big way yes, I want a divorce."

Brittany was sad for Taylor but at the same time she was glad that Taylor wasn't going to hang on for the sake of doing so. She didn't want to see her friend ran through the dirt.

"Well I think if you're not happy then you need to take the right steps to making you happy again. Don't string yourself along for nothing because that's what it sounds like.

He is done and you have done all you can to make it work Taylor. Just know that I am always here no matter what."

Taylor smiled a forced smile at Brittany.

"Thank you, Brittany. I told Blake I would get a lawyer and get the papers to him soon. You're too busy to do it so I plan on calling a lawyer in the next town. Plus, I have booked a hotel for a week so I could get away from all the fighting."

Brittany didn't like the thought of Taylor getting a lawyer from out of town and she definitely didn't like her best friend staying in a hotel while her soon to be ex stayed at their house.

"No! I will be your lawyer and you are not staying in a damn hotel Taylor! You can stay here for a week or so. It will work out great! We can work from here all week. That way you won't be at the office by yourself. Plus, we can take a few days off and hang out. We both could use the time to relax and it would save you money!"

Taylor shook her head.

"No-no-no. I'm not going to interrupt your time with lover boy. I can just stay at a hotel and work in the office. It's no big deal Britt."

"No Taylor, you can stay here. You won't interrupt us. Your room is downstairs and on the other end of the house. You will even have your own bathroom. You're staying here whether you like it or not. And you're also going to work from here with me. What's the point in you going to work and calling me on the phone when you can walk down the hall? With that settled you can run back home tonight before Blake comes home and get your stuff. Me and Michael will even ride with you!"

"Okay. I can go get some of my stuff by myself though.

Give me about an hour and I'll be back. Blake isn't going to be home for a while if at all so I don't have to worry about him."

Taylor got up to leave and almost ran into Michael.

"Oh shit, sorry!" She looked over at Brittany, "I'll be right back."

Once Taylor left, Michael sat down next to Brittany. She explained that Taylor was going to be staying with her for a week or so and they were going to work from there. She also told him about Blake and the divorce. He promised not to let on that he knew.

\*\*\*

Michael was happy that Brittany was so kind hearted with people. It was one of the many things he loved about her. He felt bad for Taylor, but was happy she had Brittany to help her out. Michael went to the kitchen to get some water and check the time. It was ten-fifteen but it felt so much later to him. He walked back into the living room and sat back next to Brittany.

"I called my mom and told her I wouldn't be home for a few days. Maybe with Taylor here I could sneak out one day next week and go check on the house. I also called Mark to tell him everything that's been going on. I also forgot to give him his key back so I asked him to come by tomorrow. I hope that's okay?"

"That's fine, babe. When is he coming over? It's supposed to be nice out tomorrow, maybe we can grill out. Afterwards, you and Mark can hang out while me and Taylor get some work done. Speaking of work, I need to call my dad tomorrow and let him know I'm not going to be in the office for a while. I'll just tell him I'm going out of town for a few days and then I'm going to stay home and catch up on some work. He won't come by unless he calls first so I'm not worried about that."

Michael loved how motivated Brittany was about her work. She loved what she did and it showed. She also loved her dad. He hated to know he could be the cause in the future for them fighting. He loved his mom and knew how much it would hurt him to hurt her.

"He is coming over around lunch so that will work out great. I was thinking maybe tomorrow we could call your friend and see about that file again. Maybe she heard something new."

Brittany nodded and scooted over closer to him. She yawned and looked up at him.

"Well, I have to get up and get the other room ready for Taylor."

He didn't want her to move. He wanted to let her relax more, but knew that was out at that moment.

"Let me help you so you can get it done faster and then you can relax."

They got up and went into the other spare room. Michael thought that door went to a closet not a room. She opened the door and turned on the lights. He liked the feeling the room gave him. It was a dark green with a dark brown trim and there were wild life pictures on the walls. One picture was a baby deer playing in an open meadow. Another picture was tall trees and a lake in the middle of a field. There was an older wooden bed frame and a dresser to match it. It was a light wood color but you could tell it was solid wood. Brittany went to another door and pulled some extra pillows out of the closet then threw them on the bed. She made sure the vent was open so the air could flow in the room.

"Michael, can you go make sure I have towels in the

other bathroom for her?"

*Another bathroom?* "Where the hell is that room hidden in this house?"

She laughed really loud and shook her head, "Come on, silly, I'll show you. You have walked by it a thousand times."

Michael was stumped then. She walked out of the room turning the light off and leaving the door open. Then she went through the living room and down the main hall. He thought she was going to turn into the office room or go out the front door but then she turned left to what he again thought was a closet. She opened the door and there it was; another bathroom. He was shocked by the color of the room. It was dark red with a black trim. It looked better then he would think a red bathroom would look. It was a nice size bathroom with a bath and shower combination. Brittany went next to the toilet to the closet where she kept towels and wash rags. Once she checked to make sure there were rags and towels in the closet, she shut the door back. From there they made their way back to the living room. They laid on the couch and waited for Taylor to come back.

\*\*\*

The mysterious man knew that Brittany had gotten his package. He watched her when she carried it in her house earlier that day. He'd stuck around until it got dark and watched when Taylor left the house. He was happy to know that they didn't call the police. *It wouldn't have mattered if they did call the police, because they would have found some way to blame Michael for it.* His new plan was coming together just fine. When they left the house earlier that day he could tell Michael was angry and Brittany was pretty shaken up. That made him happy. He wanted Michael to know he was coming. *This would shut him up once and for all. He might have made a deal with that cop last time but there wouldn't be any deals to give out this time.*

He had to go back to his hotel to get some rest. He wouldn't rest long though. He didn't need much just enough to get him ready for his next step in his plan; his final step. He figured Michael would stay close to her. He couldn't forever though. He would leave her alone at some point in time and then the mysterious man would strike. He backed away from the trees and ran back to his car. His heart was throbbing thinking about the fear in Brittany's eyes. She had no clue what was coming for her. It was all Michael's fault. He should have just kept his shit in his pants and she wouldn't be in harm's way. His mother would have met her fate but everything pointed to Brittany dying being the better option. He got in his car and pulled back onto the road. The mysterious man shook from excitement. It would all be over soon and he could finally put the past behind him for good.

*\*\**

Brittany woke up on the couch alone and wrapped up in a blanket. She must have fallen asleep while waiting on Taylor. *Oh no, Taylor! What time is it?* She reached down on the table and grabbed her phone. She had three missed calls from Taylor. She jumped up and called Taylor back.

"Everything okay?" Brittany asked as soon as Taylor answered the phone.

"No. I called because I was getting my stuff together and Blake showed up. He is in the other room now but is giving me shit about leaving. Look, I hate to ask but could you come help me get my stuff? I know you don't want to be seen with you know who but he can come and stay in the car if he wants. I just know if you're here Blake won't put up a fight with me."

Brittany instantly got mad. *Why would he put up a fight about her leaving when he has wanted to get rid of her for a while now?*

"I'll be there in a minute. Just stay in that room and pack your bag, don't come out until I get there."

She hung up and went to find Michael. She finally found him in her bathroom wearing nothing but a towel and brushing his teeth.

"As much as I would love to rip that towel off of you right now, I can't. We have to go help Taylor. Her jerk of a husband is giving her shit about leaving. You can stay in the car while I help her get her stuff. He won't fight with her if I'm there."

Michael gave her an angry face. He walked around her and to the bed where his clothes were laying on.

"So, I have to sit in the car and worry about you being around a pissed off jerk? Just promise to come out and get me if anything goes wrong, okay?"

She nodded her head and he dropped his towel. She couldn't look away.

Michael caught her looking at him and said, "Hey Britt you okay? See something you like?"

She looked up at his face and smiled.

"Of course I do, but come on we have to hurry. I'm going to grab my keys. Meet me at the door, okay?"

He nodded and she took off down the stairs to get her shoes on and grab her keys. Michael came down a few minutes later and they left for Taylor's house.

Taylor didn't live too far away. Her house was right in town. They pulled in and Brittany jumped out and ran up to the door. She didn't even knock, before she went in. Blake was on the couch watching TV, or at least looking like he was. She walked by him without speaking and went to help

Taylor. Taylor had three bags next to the door already packed.

"Taylor I'm taking these to my car. What else do you have to grab?"

Brittany looked over at Taylor and saw that she had a big black and purple eye. She had tears running down her face. Brittany dropped the bag she was holding and ran up to her. She grabbed Taylor's face and turned it to the side to show the bruises better.

"Did that mother fucker do this to you?"

Taylor looked down and didn't speak. All she did was nod.

"I'll be right back, Taylor. Keep packing and don't come out of this room until I tell you to. You got it?"

Taylor nodded and kept packing. Brittany saw red and was ready to let the devil out of the bag. She walked into the living room and picked the remote off the table turning the TV.

"I'm going to give you a chance to answer me honestly. How many beers have you had? Are you beyond drunk?"

Blake looked up at her with dark eyes.

"I don't remember how much I had but it was a lot. Why are you even here, Brittany?"

Blake's words were slurred and all over the place. She knew he was drunk and wouldn't remember that night at all; which is what she wanted. He wouldn't be able to id anyone being as drunk as he was. She walked out the front door and didn't bother to shut it behind her. Michael jumped out of the car as if he could tell something was wrong.

"I want you to come with me Michael. Just promise not to kill him okay?"

He nodded and she could almost see the color of his eyes change from anger. She walked him inside past Blake into Taylor's room. Taylor looked up when the door opened. Brittany saw Michael's fist ball up and she knew what was about to happen and she was just fine with it.

# CHAPTER FOURTEEN

ichael's heart dropped when he saw Brittany come out the door without bags in her hand. Something was wrong and he knew it. He didn't even wait for her to tell him to get out. She asked him to promise not to kill someone and he wasn't sure he could keep that promise if someone hurt her. She walked him in the house and he saw a drunken guy on the couch. They walked by him and went into another room. He didn't understand what was wrong. When the door opened, he saw why Brittany came and got him. His fist instantly went into a tight ball. He didn't know Taylor very well but he did know that she was someone Brittany really cared about.

He looked back at Brittany and said, "Get her stuff together and get it in the car now, Brittany."

He watched the girls carry out five luggage bags, attempting to contain himself. Brittany stopped in the door way.

"Michael don't kill him; I'm trusting you."

"You get in the car with Taylor and I'll take your car. Wait on me and we will leave together," he replied without looking at her.

She didn't argue and closed the door behind her. The TV was on then and the guy Michael assumed was Blake was so out of it he didn't even notice Michael. Michael went over and grabbed Blake's beer and threw it into the TV. Blake jumped up and got in Michael's face.

"What the fuck do you think you're doing? Who the fuck are you anyway?"

"I'm the guy that comes to see you when you hit women. If you touch another woman. I promise I'll do way more to you then what I'm about to do."

Michael pulled his arm back and hit Blake right in the jaw. Blake didn't say a word he just fell right on the coffee table and didn't move. Michael knew he knocked him out and might have broken his jaw, but he didn't care. He walked out of the house closing the door behind him. He looked over at Brittany in the driver seat of Taylor's car. He went to the window and got her keys not saying a word. Michael drove off first and Brittany followed.

They got back to Brittany's house and Michael opened both the girl's doors.

"Britt, get her inside and I'll grab the bags."

The girls walked inside and Michael got all the bags in one trip. He toted them to the spare room. The girls were sitting on the couch talking so he gave them some space. He ran upstairs to Brittany's bathroom first and grabbed a first aid kit he saw under the sink. He got a rag and wet it with cold water. Back in the kitchen, he got down two glasses and poured the girls some wine. He walked into the living room and sat down the wine. Brittany was smiling up at him. He handed her the first aid kit then handed the rag to Taylor.

"Put that on your eye for a little while and once the swelling goes down put on some cream from the first aid kit. There should be an instant ice pack in there too. Wrap the rag around it and that should help a lot."

Taylor stared at Michael, gratefully.

"I'm going to give y'all a chance to talk. I'm going to make me a sundae. Do y'all want one too?"

They both smiled at him. Taylor spoke first, "Brittany, you have an amazing guy. You better not let him go. I was so wrong about you Michael. Oh, and I'll take some ice cream please."

"I'll take one too if you don't mind babe."

He nodded and walked back to the kitchen. He didn't think he was anything special. As far as he was concerned, all he did was help someone out. They make it out like he was a hero. He didn't understand it but he was just happy to see them both smile.

After they all ate some ice cream they parted ways and went to bed. Once in the bed with Brittany, Michael kissed her on the head and she was soon fast asleep. He was never the type of person to be able to fall asleep right as he laid down. He always used that time to think about things. He hoped the next day would be a better day and the girls could relax. Mark was coming by for a while and he always knew how to make women laugh. Maybe that would take their minds off everything. Michael ran his fingers through Brittany's hair until he finally fell asleep.

*** 

Brittany woke up to an empty bed and the light shining in the bedroom. *Michael must be downstairs,* she thought as she went to pee and brush her teeth. Afterwards she headed down to find him. He had made breakfast again. She smiled as she made a mental note to make sure she cooked breakfast for him and did something special for him. He deserved it after everything thing he had done for her so far. He stared up at her as he sipped on some coffee. She walked to the table and got a glass of orange juice then sat down next to him. He reached over and grabbed her hand then kissed it.

"Is Taylor not up yet?"

"Yeah she got up a while ago and said she was going to take a shower. I'm guessing she should be out soon."

She drank some of her juice then looked at the table of food. Michael made waffles, sausage, eggs, and toast. He had coffee, milk, and orange juice laid out to drink. He knew how to make a great breakfast.

"Thank you for cooking for me again! I promise to cook dinner tonight to make it up to you."

"You're welcome and do you mind if I helped you cook? I think it would be a lot of fun," he said with a laugh.

Just then Taylor opened the bathroom door and looked over at them. Brittany noticed that she had on more makeup then she normally wore. Her heart ached for Taylor, because the makeup didn't cover the bruises up too well. Brittany remembered she had some foundation that she knew would cover the bruises all the way up.

"Taylor come eat. Michael made breakfast."

"You mean he can cook, too? Do you have any single brothers?"

Taylor laughed and sat down at the table. Michael started making his plate, and then looked up at Taylor.

"I don't have any brothers but I do have a single friend who is pretty much my brother."

Taylor poured herself some coffee.

"Well one day you should introduce me to him."

Brittany laughed knowing she would meet him sooner

than Taylor thought.

\*\*\*

Michael sat in the living room waiting on Mark to call. It was around twelve thirty and the girls were in the office working. They'd helped him clean up and then Brittany took Taylor up to her room to help her cover up her bruises better. When Taylor came back down he couldn't even tell she was bruised. Michael couldn't understand why women wore makeup. If it could cover up bruises, then what else could it hide? Michael's phone started ringing and he jumped up to answer it.

"Hello?"

"Hey, I'm near the farm where do I turn at?"

Michael told him which drive way and hung up the phone. He passed the office where the girls were talking and working. The door to the office was opened and they stopped talking when he passed and went out the door. Michael walked onto the porch. He heard a soft rustle behind him, so he looked back over his shoulder. He almost laughed out loud when he saw the girls crack open the door so they could see what was going on. Mark pulled up behind Taylor's car and parked. Michael walked over to Mark's truck still smirking.

Michael and Mark did their normal handshake, and then Michael stood back and whispered to Mark, "We have eyes on us."

Mark looked over and the door shut really fast. They both laughed.

"Is someone else here other then you and Brittany?"

"Yeah Brittany's best friend is staying with her for a while. She had some issues with her soon to be ex and is going to camp out here for a while. Plus, the girls work together so they are going to work from here. Come on in so you can meet the stalkers."

Mark chuckled and followed Michael inside. Michael shut the door behind Mark and walked to the office. He laughed when he saw the girls acting like they were working and not paying them any attention.

"Ladies this is my friend Mark. Mark this is Brittany and Taylor," Michael said as he pointed to each one as he said their names.

"Nice to meet y'all."

The girls stared at Mark for a second before Brittany finally answered, "We are happy to meet you too, Mark. Michael, we are going to finish up this report and then we will get the food ready to cook." Michael nodded and walked to the kitchen with Mark following. Michael got Mark a beer out of the fridge and handed it to him.

"We are going to do some grilling. Want to hang out for a while?"

"Heck yeah man. I'm starving."

Michael opened the back door to see where the grill was at. He walked out on the porch to look around. He'd never been out back and had no idea it would look like it did out there. The porch on the back was huge and open. It had a table and chairs on one end and a grill with a small bar on the other. In the middle of the porch there was a huge tree where she had the porch built around it. The really cool thing was she had a flower bed and benches around the base of the tree on the porch.

Mark whistled, "Dude, she has an amazing place."

Mark was right; it was amazing. Once they walked off

the porch, the yard was open until it faded into a tree line off in the distance. Brittany had a bird bath, a fountain, and a pond. She even had flower beds all around the house. Michael noticed something in the corner of her yard and walked over to see what it was. Once he got near the tree line he noticed it was a deer decoy. He was shocked, he knew she was a country girl but had no idea she hunted. She had the decoy set up and even another target set up beside it. There was a small shack next to the decoys with a big lock on the outside. He wondered what was in it. Brittany surprised him more and more.

"Dude she hunts? This is your dream woman all the way!"

Michael laughed because he knew that before he found the decoy; that was just a bonus.

"I already know, man. I already know. Let's go start up the grill and get the girls to help us out," he said before they walked back to the house.

***

Brittany and Taylor finished the report they were working on and headed to the kitchen. Brittany saw the guys outside as she started grabbing food to be cooked on the grill. She handed Taylor the chicken and barbeque sauce.

"I saw the way you looked at Mark. It's funny how you can always talk to any guy, but you couldn't even say a word when he walked in. Want to tell me why?"

Taylor got down a plate out of the cabinet and searched for tongs.

"I just didn't know what to say to him. Don't read into it too much, I have too much going on right now to worry about another guy."

Brittany understood that, so she let the subject drop. She knew Taylor might not need another guy in her life but that didn't mean it wouldn't happen. She could see something in both Taylor and Mark's eyes that made her think of her and Michael.

Brittany started taking the food outside. She walked over to the grill and saw Michael and Mark walking back to the porch. She figured they had spotted her decoys and the shack. It was another hobby of hers. She liked to hunt when she had the time. Unfortunately, she hadn't been able to get out because of her workload. When Brittany was a little girl she would go on hunting trips with her dad all the time. They always brought some kind of meat home with them. She loved hunting; there was something about being in nature that made her feel complete.

Brittany pulled the cover off the grill and attempted to light it up. Michael came over and helped her light the grill. "Don't worry babe, Mark and I will take care of the grilling. You and Taylor relax."

After all the food Michael had cooked her the past few days, she wasn't about to let him cook that meal too.

"No. You have made me breakfast two times now. It's my turn to cook. Why don't you and Mark set up the bar and make everyone a drink. There is a cooler in the bar. Just put some beer in it for you two. If you look above the stove in the cabinet, there are all different types of alcohol. Just pick something and make us a fruity drink."

She smiled at Michael and went back to setting up the grill. Michael went inside and Mark followed. Taylor watched the guys through the window in the kitchen.

"Okay, so what's up Taylor? You're never this quiet."

Taylor sighed and looked over at Brittany.

"I don't know how to explain it. I feel like a big weight has been lifted off my shoulders. Being here for only one night has made such a difference. I don't need Blake in my life anymore. I don't want him in it anymore. I haven't even thought about him until you brought it up a little bit ago. I almost felt guilty for not thinking of him all day but then something told me I needed to worry about me and not him for once. I want what you and Michael have and maybe one day I'll find it. For now, I'm going to have fun and be me."

Brittany had never been happier to hear her friend say that. Taylor put some barbeque sauce on the chicken while Brittany set it on the grill. They had some corn wrapped up in aluminum foil with butter inside of it. Brittany set it on the top rack of the grill along with some potatoes wrapped in aluminum foil. She closed the grill and placed the tongs on the plate. They flipped the chicken every so often and talked about work a little.

Once the guys came outside they joined in the conversation. Brittany and Michael laughed as Taylor talked about her family coming for a visit the following year. Taylor never got along with her family so they had always been a big joke between Brittany and Taylor. Mark couldn't take his eyes off of Taylor. Brittany and Michael noticed at the same time and gave each other the same look. Brittany took a sip of the drink Michael made her. It was sweet and tangy at the same time. She could taste the orange juice and what seemed to be pineapple vodka in it.

Michael and Mark went and sat at the table on the other side of the porch.

"Go ahead, Taylor, I'm just going to flip these one more time and then I'll come sit down too."

Taylor went and sat beside Mark while Brittany flipped the chicken. Once she was done, she closed the grill top and went over to sit down next to Michael. Brittany could tell that the conversation must have taken a serious tone because everyone was frowning and looking at her. She looked at Michael.

"What's wrong?"

"Just catching Mark up on what's going on."

"Oh, about the crazy person."

Brittany was tired of dealing with it already. Why did someone need to frame Michael so bad? What did Michael do for someone to hate him so much? None of it made any since to her. Mark spoke and snapped her back to the conversation.

"So, who could it be man?"

Michael only shrugged his shoulders. Brittany could see how bad he was hurting over everything. She hated seeing him so upset and not being able to help him.

"Well I think the food is done. If you two want to grab some plates, we can eat out here if y'all want."

Brittany and Taylor walked over to the grill.

"Taylor, will you grab me some butter and cheese out of the fridge for the potatoes?"

"Sure. Do you need anything else?"

"Can you get my platter out so I can place the potatoes and corn on it?"

Taylor nodded and headed to the kitchen as Michael and Mark placed the plates and forks on the table. Everyone sat down and ate while talking and laughing. Taylor and Mark had a lot in common. They both had the same taste in music, sports, and even TV shows. Brittany could tell they liked each other more than they were probably willing to admit.

They sat outside most of the day just talking. Taylor and Mark volunteered to clean off the table so Brittany and Michael cleaned the grill.

"So, what's in the shed over there? Oh, and you never told me you like to hunt." Michael said to Brittany.

Brittany laughed, "You never asked. There are a few garden tools and a few of my trophy racks hanging up in there. I used to go on hunting trips with my dad. I managed to get a few good-sized bucks so I kept their antlers and hung them up in the shack."

Michael's mouth dropped.

"What's wrong?"

He didn't say anything for a minute. Brittany finished cleaning off the grill.

"Oh, come on I'll show you. Just let me grab my key and I'll meet you out there."

Brittany went inside and found Mark and Taylor having a water fight. She slipped by them and went to grab her key. She didn't want them to stop having fun on her account so she tried to be unseen. Once she got her key, she went back outside to meet Michael at the shed.

# CHAPTER FIFTEEN

M ichael waited by the shed for Brittany to get the key. In all the mess going on around them, he found it great how they could still make each other smile. Everyday his feelings for her grew. He wondered if they would have found each other if he wasn't being framed. He was glad he made the discussion to ask for Brittany's help. If he hadn't then he would have never been able to get that close to her. In a twisted way, the killer brought them together, and now was trying to rip them apart. He wasn't going to let that happen in his lifetime.

Michael spotted Brittany walking across the yard towards him. He had a mental image of her as his wife walking down the aisle. His mind told him to slow down but his heart wanted him to jump at every chance and love her like she needed.

Brittany unlocked the door and turned on a light inside. The building was small but big enough to fit about four people in. He walked in and looked around. On one wall, she had all her garden tools hanging up. On the floor under them she had a leaf blower and a weed eater. Next to that her lawn mower was parked. He walked over to the other wall where she had about ten antlers hanging all over the wall. She had killed bucks of all sizes; from only a spike up to a twelve-point buck. For a second Michael felt like he was in a man's shed. Then he realized it was too organized to be a guy's. He turned around looking at Brittany.

"This is amazing, Britt. You sure have gotten some big ones over the years. Maybe me and you could go hunting later this year after everything is cleared up." He knew it would have to be after his record was clean, because he couldn't get a hunting license until it was.

"Maybe," Brittany said as she walked over to the spike horn and pointed at it. "This was the first buck I got when I was ten. I had shot a doe the year before. I was so happy when I got him." She went to the huge twelve point and pulled it off the wall. "This was the last buck I got. I went with my dad on a hunting trip a few years back in South Carolina. I saw him one day but couldn't get a shot at him. I thought he wouldn't come back, but the next day he did and I was able to get a shot off. My dad and I spent hours looking for him. I shot him in the shoulder so he didn't go down right off. He went about a mile before dying. It's amazing how strong these animals are, God made them tough for a reason. We don't kill them for trophies; we kill them to eat them. Some people seem to have a problem with hunters because they kill for trophies and not food. Me and my dad always thanked God for our kills and prayed every time we got one."

"That's amazing, Britt. I wish I had a dad to do that stuff with. Growing up I loved hunting, I would always go with my mom's brother. I shot my first deer when I was seven, it was a doe. I shot my first buck when I was eleven. It was my favorite thing to do, until I got put in prison anyways. My uncle died while I was locked up. I figured I wouldn't ever hunt again, but maybe me and you can make it our thing one day."

Brittany smiled at him and walked out of the shed. He followed her and she locked it behind him. They walked back up the porch hand in hand. Michael opened the door to let Brittany go in first. They walked into the kitchen and didn't see Mark or Taylor. *Wonder where they went.* Brittany gave him the same look and they walked into the living room. They found Taylor and Mark sitting on the couch talking. They sat down and joined in on the conversation. Everyone drank and ate snacks while they talked and watched a movie.

Mark looked at Michael, "Well dude, I guess I should head out. I know y'all are tired and I don't want to intrude."

Mark got up as if to head for the door. Michael didn't want him to drive since he had a few beers. Michael looked at Brittany. She spoke before Michael could. "Why don't you crash here, Mark? It won't be intruding on us at all. Plus, you have been drinking. I don't want you to wreck or get pulled over."

Mark looked at Michael before he sighed and said, "I guess you're right. Are you sure you don't mind?"

"No not at all! Let me get a pillow and some blankets out of Taylor's closet."

Brittany went into Taylor's room and Taylor headed behind her after saying, "I'm going to change. I'll be right back."

Brittany came out a few minutes later with a pillow and a thick blanket. She laid them both on the side of the couch. "Feel free to watch TV and if you get hungry or thirsty help yourself. I have Netflix too so if you find a good movie feel free to watch it."

Taylor walked out of her room in a t-shirt and shorts and made her way back to the couch.

Michael stood up. "Well I guess we're going to head to bed. Does anyone need to be up at a certain time tomorrow?"

Taylor and Mark both shook their head. Mark looked at Taylor. "I'm not really tired. Want to watch a movie with me?"

Taylor crossed her legs on the couch and said, "Sure, sounds good."

Michael and Brittany said goodnight and headed to bed. Michael caught a glance at the clock. It was only nine thirty and he wasn't too tired himself, but he wanted to spend some time with Brittany alone. Once in Brittany's room, Michael grabbed her hand. "I'm going to grab a quick shower. If you want, you can join me. I promise not to try anything. I actually wanted to talk to you about some stuff tonight."

Brittany looked down at the floor. "No, that's okay. You go ahead. I'll take one after you do."

Michael knew the reason why she didn't want to shower with him was because of her stomach. He hated that she was so self-conscious. He didn't understand why she was so shy about it. "Britt, I won't look at your stomach if you don't want me to. I just want you to know that you are beautiful to me no matter what. Just trust me okay?"

She stood there looking at the floor for a while not answering. Finally she spoke, "Okay, but let me get in first then you can come in okay?"

Michael nodded. Brittany walked in the bathroom and shut the door behind her. He waited five or so minutes and then went in. The steam from the shower had already started to fog up the mirror. He undressed and put his clothes in a neat pile on the floor. He opened the shower door and got in. Brittany had her back to him and was facing the water stream. Michael moved close enough to her that the water would spray on him too.

He found her shampoo and started to wash her hair. She laid her head back to let him scrub her head. He thought he heard her moan a little, it made him smile. He let her rinse her hair under the spray of water. Brittany reached down and grabbed a bottle of conditioner. He took the bottle from her and put some in his hands. He rubbed the conditioner in her hair just like the shampoo. This time while she rinsed it out he found her sponge and two bottles of body wash. He smelt the first one, it was a lavender scent. The second one smelled sweet so he went with that one. He lathered the sponge up and washed her shoulders. She jumped at first but soon gave in still facing away from him. He washed her back and arms then moved down to her butt and legs. He planted a soft kiss on her butt cheek before standing back up.

He put his lips up to her ear, "Britt, can you please turn around? I'll let the water spray in my face and wash you blind. Just please let me do this."

Brittany looked down and nodded. She stepped forward and let the water spray in his face. Michael quickly realized it was going to be harder then he planned, but he was determined to do it. He thought if he did this then it might help Brittany trust him.

"You might have to guide me at first Britt because I can't see."

Brittany grabbed his hands and placed them on what he could tell was her shoulders. He washed her arms and neck. He ran his free hand down one of her breast and used the other hand to wash it. Once he was finished he moved to the other breast. Afterwards, he trailed his free hand to her stomach, bent down, and washed her stomach. Then he used his free hand to guide himself to washing her legs. He ran his hand back up to the top of her thigh and nudged her legs hoping she would open them. He squeezed soap on his hands from the sponge. Laying the sponge on the ground he guided his hand to her thigh. He washed all over her enchanted garden before he ran his fingers around her folds. She moaned a little, but he stopped to hold true to his promise to not start anything. He stood back up and wiped his eyes. By the time he opened them, Brittany had already turned around to rinse herself. Michael hoped his gesture was a step in the right direction. He truly wanted her to understand how beautiful she was to him and how perfect her body was.

Brittany got done rinsing her body and stepped out of the shower. Michael washed his hair and body and also got out. He wasn't surprised to see that Brittany had already dressed by the time he got out. She gave him an endearing look as she brushed her teeth. He smiled and walked past her to the bedroom. He got dressed and then brushed his teeth. When he got in bed, Brittany was sitting up on the edge brushing her hair.

"Thank you for doing that. It helped me more then you know. I had trouble with weight for a while. I got really big then really small. When I was big I couldn't control my stretch marks so that's why I won't let you see my stomach. I hate it; it's the worst part about my body. I can't stand to look at them and I don't want you to have to either."

"Are you crazy, Britt? You think some marks on your body make you ugly? I love every inch of your body; including your stretch marks. You might not like to look at them but I don't mind them at all. I have scars all over my body. Trust me when I say this Britt, I love every part of you; inside and out."

She smiled at him for a second and then looked away before changing the subject. "So, what did you want to talk about?"

"It's about us and this being out in public together business. I don't want to fight Britt but I just want to know something." He sighed and looked up at her big blue eyes, "Look I love you Britt, and I just want to know if we will always hide it from the world. I only bring it up again because it bothers me so much. I loved being with our friends today. It was nice to be able to show you off to someone. I just don't want it to always be behind closed doors. I feel like you're ashamed to be with me and that's why you don't want to be seen with me. Why should it matter what everyone else thinks as long as we are happy? I guess I say that because I'm not the type of person to care what anyone else thinks. So I don't get why you are. It just hurts Britt."

He could see he flipped a switch. She went from happy to angry in seconds. "It hurts that you think I am ashamed of you. I honestly don't know how long it will be like this. However, I do know this is just how it has to be for a while. I don't usually care about what people think of me but as a lawyer, my reputation matters with my job. My dad's opinion matters to me too and you should know that. He would never forgive me for being with you. To him you're a murder and even though we both know it's not true we still don't have proof. I get that you want to be in public with me and I want that too but there is more at stake here then what we want. It hurts that you won't even look at it from my side. I don't want you to sit around here with me if you can't handle being hidden for a while. I don't want to lose you because I love you a lot Michael, but it sounds like you aren't sure what you want."

He went to respond back to her but she held up her hand to him. She didn't want to hear anything he had to say. She laid down and rolled over on her side away from him. He was angry at what she said so he got up and left the room. He wasn't going to stay somewhere he wasn't welcome, but he wasn't going to leave the person he loved alone and in danger so he decided to sleep in the office.

He stopped in the kitchen to pour him something to drink. Mark was in there making himself a sandwich. "What's wrong man? You look pissed?"

Michael opened the fridge and got out a soda. "It's a long story man. Anyway, what are you doing tomorrow?"

Mark started putting up the sandwich meat. "Nothing until I go into work at three. Why? What do you need?"

"I need to go check on my mom's house. Do you mind hanging around until I get back? If you do have to leave, you can. Taylor will be here so Britt should be okay. I don't think crazy guy will show up with someone else here."

Mark nodded and took a bite of his sandwich. "Sure man."

Michael said goodnight and headed for the office. When he walked by the living room, he saw that Taylor was still on the couch curled up with a blanket. He was glad to see that her and Mark were getting along good. Maybe a little too good but it wasn't his business. It took Michael a while to get comfortable. He hated sleeping without Brittany, but he refused to sleep next to her that night. Plus, she didn't even want him around her. He would leave early in the morning so she would have time to think about everything. He finally fell asleep wishing Brittany was beside him.

# CHAPTER SIXTEEN

**B**rittany didn't sleep well that night without Michael. She missed him and he wasn't even really gone. She wondered where he slept at, thinking he might have slept on the couch in her office. She got dressed and brushed her teeth and made her way down the stairs. Once downstairs she went to see if everyone was still asleep. There wasn't any breakfast in the kitchen like she'd gotten accustomed to, so she knew Michael was still mad at her. In the living room, Taylor and Mark were asleep on the couch. She went to see if Michael was asleep in the office. The door was open but he wasn't in there. Just then she heard his truck start up. *He's leaving.* Her heart broke a little. *Are we done? I shouldn't have said what I did. Maybe I didn't completely see it from his side.*

Brittany walked back to the kitchen with a sick feeling in her stomach. If being public was a deal breaker, would she be able to bend a little and give into what he wanted? She didn't know for sure, but she did know that she loved Michael and didn't want to lose him over a stupid fight. She went to get her some orange juice out of the fridge and saw a note attached to a magnet.

*Brittany,*

*I went to go check on my mom's house. Mark and Taylor will keep you company while I'm gone. I'm sorry about last night and I regret bringing it up. We will talk when I get back.*

*Keep your phone on you so I can check in.*

*Always,*
*Michael*

Brittany felt a little bit of her broken heart fall back into place knowing that Michael was coming back. She drank her orange juice and sat at the table. She knew she had to make things right with Michael. Maybe she should talk to her dad and tell him what's going on. He was an understanding person wasn't he? Maybe, but she didn't think he would be about Michael. She had to give it a try for Michael though.

Brittany heard her phone ringing upstairs, thinking it was Michael she ran up to grab it. She missed the call by the time she got to her room. When she looked at her phone, the call was from Christine. Brittany crossed her fingers that it was good news about what was going on with the file. She called her back and waited for Christine to answer.

"Hey Brittany I was just leaving you a voice mail. I got a hold of someone who can open the file. The thing with it is that it can only be opened on the computer that opens those types of files. So, he will have to come to you or you go to him. He said he can fly to you in two days but that's the best he could do."

"Okay so if I decide to go to him, where is he located?"

Christine paused, which led Brittany to believe that she was going to be letting him come to her.

"He is in Russia."

"Yeah, just let him come to me because there is no way I'm going to Russia."

Brittany ended her conversation and sent Michael a text. *Christine called. Guy is coming to open the file in two days. Will explain more when you get here.*

Brittany walked back down to the kitchen. Taylor was in there making her some food.

"Well morning sunshine," Brittany said with a smirk.

Taylor laughed and went back to cooking. Brittany could tell Taylor was in a better mood.

Brittany's phone pinged with a message.

*I might not be back for a bit. Mom is back home and wants me to explain what's going on. I can't lie to her anymore so I have to talk to her. I'll be back as soon as I can.*

That sucked, but she understood. At least she had Mark and Taylor to keep her company. Taylor sat down with her food and started to eat the omelet she made.

"So, is Michael still sleeping?"

Brittany knew that Taylor read the note and knew Michael was gone. She was just trying to find a way to talk about their fight.

"No, he had to go check on his mom. He will be back later."

Taylor took a bite of food, and said, "I went to the bathroom in the middle of the night and I saw Michael in the office. Why was he sleeping in there? Did y'all have a fight?"

Brittany sighed and stood up, "Yeah, it was stupid. He slept on the couch and left early this morning before I woke up," Brittany paused as she went to the refrigerator. She picked out a strawberry yogurt and went back to the table.

"He is upset about me not wanting to be seen in public with him. I know it sounds bad, but I have a reputation to uphold. I can't be seen with a criminal. Even if he really isn't one, everyone else thinks he is."

Taylor's mouth fell open. "You said it like that to him?"

Brittany just nodded. "Well I can see why he slept on the couch then. Look at it this way Brittany. Is it so wrong that he wants to show you off? I can see what you mean by not wanting to mess up your reputation but girl you only find love once. Is your reputation worth losing him?"

"I know. Taylor and I have given it some thought. I am going to talk to my dad today and let him know a little bit about what's going on. He will freak out but I want to show Michael that I'm not ashamed of him. I'm just hoping that by telling my dad it will show Michael I'm making steps in the right direction that he wants."

"Just let me know when your dad is coming by for that conversation because I don't want to be here for that. I think it will help things with you and Michael though." She smiled and finished with her omelet.

Once Brittany finished her yogurt she got up, threw away the container, and went to the living room. She passed Mark on her way.

"Good morning, Brittany. Is it okay if I take a quick shower?"

"Of course, there are towels in the closet in the bathroom. If you want you can use Michael's soap, all that is in there is girly stuff. I can run up and grab it for you if you want?"

"Sure, that would be great if you don't mind."

She shook her head and ran up to her bathroom. She grabbed Michael's soap, she headed back down to hand it to Mark. Mark was on the phone when she reached him. Brittany noticed he looked bothered. He hung up the phone with a look of concern on his face.

"Is everything okay?" she asked.

"No, I have to go. My mom fell and needs me. I'll call Mike and let him know I had to go. You should be okay with Taylor here, plus he should be back soon."

Mark ran in the living room and kissed Taylor on the cheek then took off out the door. Brittany went and made sure the door was locked and went back to see Taylor. "Well that tells me why you have been smiling all morning." Taylor blushed for the first time in forever and Brittany knew she was in deep with Mark.

Brittany got her laptop out of her office and then went back in the living room with Taylor. "Did you by any chance grab the list of numbers and client names from your desk?" Without them she couldn't call any of her clients.

Taylor looked up in shock, "No, I didn't know you weren't coming back to work. I can run and grab them really quick if you want. It won't take me but thirty minutes tops."

Brittany was a little skittish about being left alone, but Taylor was right it wouldn't be for more than thirty minutes.

"Yeah, just run and grab them. While you're there can you go in my office and get the stack of old case files on my desk? I have to look through them for Mrs. Jenkins but I forgot them."

Taylor nodded and went to her room to change. Brittany kept working as much as she could without the names and numbers. Dressed and ready to go, Taylor came out of her room with her keys in hand.

"I'll be right back Brittany. Just lock the door behind me okay?"

Brittany got up and followed Taylor to the door and locked it behind her. It was the first time in a few days she had been alone and it gave her an eerie feeling. She went back to the living room and sat on the couch; getting back to work so she wouldn't worry about being alone. A few minutes later she had to stop working because she didn't have what she needed to finish. She decided to run upstairs and get some clothes together to do laundry. She knew Michael needed some things washed so it made sense. It was a weird thought to be doing their laundry together, but it was a good weird. She gathered up the clothes out of the bathroom and her bedroom hamper.

She was about to turn and go down the steps when she heard something click. It sounded like a lock but she wasn't sure. Just then she had a cold chill run up her spine. She backed away from the stairs to hide. She poked her head around the corner to see if she could see anything. For a second she thought her mind was tricking her but quickly realized it wasn't. She saw a man with a hood over his head slowly walk by the stairs. Brittany almost screamed, but luckily halted the instinct to do so. She tried to stay calm but her heart was racing like never before. She backed up slowly and went to her room and shut the door as quiet as she could. Thanking God that she had put a lock on the door as she twisted the lock. She took her phone and went to the bathroom. She got in the tub and laid down pulling the curtain closed around her.

She texted Michael: *The killer is here. I'm in the bath tub hiding. Hurry.*

# CHAPTER SEVENTEEN

Brittany dialed 911. She waited for them to answer and then hung up; knowing that the operator would send help. She turned her phone on silent and laid as still as she could. She almost forgot to breath she was so scared. Just as she got her breathing under control she heard her bedroom door knob rattle. *Damn!* She didn't even have a weapon to protect herself. At that point she couldn't get to her closet in time to grab a gun. She looked down at her phone. 911 tried to call her back and Michael texted her. She read his text. *Don't move. I'm coming. Brittany prayed that Michael or the police showed up to save her.* She almost jumped out of her skin when she heard the intruder trying to break her bedroom door down. After a few failed attempts, she heard clicking noises as he tried to pick the door lock. Brittany knew she was in trouble. She sent Michael a text back knowing it would be her last words to him, because there was no way he would get to her in time. *I love you Michael and I'm sorry about last night. Just know that I love you so much. He is in my room now. I don't have long and I know it. Pray for me.* She hit send and she started to shake.

She heard the intruder cuss and then the door slowly creaked open. She felt like she was going to have a heart attack she was so scared. She started to pray in her head hoping God would let a miracle happen. She could hear him walking around in her room. Then there wasn't any sound at all. Did he leave? No, she knew better than that. The intruder made his way to the bathroom door and shook the door knob. She was really shaking by then. So many things ran through her mind. She didn't want to die. She wanted to be with Michael, get married, and have kids. She wanted to see her dad again and hug him tight. She also worried that Michael would get framed for her murder too and spend the rest of his life in prison. No, she had to fight back; scratch him and get some DNA under her nails, something. She wasn't going to go down without a fight so she stood up quietly and waited for him to get through the lock on the door.

Just as the door opened and she was about to attack she heard Michael yell out in her room. "You picked the wrong time today, mother fucker." Brittany's heart sank. She was stuck to the spot she was in and couldn't bring herself to move. She was so scared not only for her but now for Michael too. She heard a fight break out in her room. Her brain wouldn't tell her body to move no matter how hard she tried. She heard a loud breaking noise and she was a whole new scared. Was Michael hurt? She had to make sure he was okay. She forced herself to move. She readied herself to attack if she had to, but when she got to her room no one was there. Michael and the intruder were both gone. The window in her room was shattered. She ran to the window hoping Michael wasn't hurt on the ground outside. As she looked out the window she cut her arm, but she didn't care because she was worried about Michael. Neither of the two were on the ground. *What the hell is going on?*

Just as she was about to look away, she saw Michael running after someone in the tree line. She hoped he would catch him but was also worried that he might get hurt by him. Brittany raced down the stairs and locked the door back. She leaned against the door and took a deep breath as the reality of what just happened completely sunk in. She lost time as she stood there with tears trickling from her eyes. It wasn't until Brittany heard sirens that her tears stopped falling. She had forgotten that she called the cops.

*Good thing Michael came when he did because I would have been dead by the time they got here.* When the cops got to the door, she opened it. Two cops rushed in with guns drawn with Taylor behind them. Brittany explained what happened and one cop took off in the woods and the other two stayed back.

\*\*\*

Michael was deep into the woods and out of breath. The house wasn't behind him anymore so he hoped he would be able to find his way back. The man bobbed and weaved in the woods like it was his home. Michael lost sight of the man when his pants got snagged on a brier. All Michael could do was cuss under his breath and feel like a failure. He pulled on his pants and turned back in the direction he thought the house was in. He hurried so he could make sure Brittany was okay.

Michael almost got turned around a few times as he ran through the woods. It wasn't until he heard the sirens that he knew he was close. He moved toward the noise and finally saw the house poke through the tree line. Brittany was on the porch with two cops when Michael got to the field. His eyes met Brittany's. She pushed her way past the cops and ran over to him. He pulled her into a hug and heard her sob into his shoulder. He held her for a minute before he pushed her away from him to look down at her. He brushed the tears from her face.

"Britt, I am so sorry I left you today. I never should have left you. I am the reason you were put in danger and I'll never forgive myself. If anything would have happened to you today, I would have lost it."

Michael could feel his throat get tight so he stopped talking. He knew he was about to cry so he pulled her back into a hug. He felt anger wash over him because whoever was trying to frame him had made the worst mistake of their life. No one was going to hurt Brittany and he would make damn sure of that.

***

It was an hour later and Michael sat with Brittany as she wrote her statement. She handed the officer her statement once she finished with it.

The officer looked at Michael. "We need you to give me your statement too. Take your time and write down every detail you can. Do you think you could identify the guy?"

Michael took the paper and pen from the officer. "No. He had a hood on most of the time until we fought. Even when we fought, I still didn't see much of his face. It was like he had leather on his face or something. I know he was wearing a wig though; it moved when I hit him. I think he knew he was going to lose the fight, so he just got up and jumped out the damn window like Superman. I tried to grab him but he slipped away. When I got outside, he was running to the tree line. It was like he knew the woods because he zigged and zagged his way through the trees. I lost him when it got too thick."

He looked over at Brittany "I'm sorry Britt, I should've had him. I'm so sorry." Brittany felt so bad for him in that moment. He looked down at the paper and started to write his statement. She wanted to comfort him right then but there were too many cops around. Brittany put her face in her hands and wished it was all a dream. She heard a familiar voice at her door. She looked up to see her dad standing at the door talking to one of the officers. Brittany knew it was going to be bad. She got up and went to the front door to calm her dad down before he saw Michael.

***

Michael looked up from his statement when Brittany got up and headed to the front door. *Great, her dad is here. This*

153

*day is getting better and better by the minute,* he thought when he saw Officer Johnson. He looked back down at his paper and finished his statement. When he was done, Michael got up from the table and went to the living room to avoid her dad. He wanted to be there to help Brittany talk to him but he knew he would only make it worse. When he got in the living room, Taylor was in there with an officer.

Michael sat on the couch and put his head down in his hands. His mind wandered around the day. He shouldn't have left Brittany that morning, but he had to talk to his mom and make sure she was okay. He couldn't keep her in the dark any longer. He didn't think both Mark and Taylor would have left Brittany alone. Thinking back, he could still remember when he got the text from Brittany about the killer being there. His heart stopped and he forgot to breath. He was already on his way back to Brittany's house but he still had a good ten minutes before he would get there. He remembered hitting the gas and pushing the truck to go as fast as it could. When he got to Brittany's house, he walked as quiet as he could. By the time he got up to Brittany's room, the guy had gotten the bathroom door open. Michael knew if he was even a few seconds later the guy would have gotten to Brittany and that messed him up.

Taylor brought Michael out of his memory. "Are you okay, Michael? Your head is bleeding and you have a bruise on your cheek." He didn't even know he was hurt. He touched his head and sure enough his head was bleeding. He looked back up for Taylor but she was gone. She came back seconds later with a first aid kit. He took it from her and snapped the instant ice pack then placed it on his cheek.

"You're going to need stitches, Michael. I'll go grab one of the medics before they leave." Before he could tell her no she was already gone. He heard her yell out the front door for the medic.

He heard what he thought was Taylor coming back in the living room but it was really Brittany. "Are you okay? I didn't even notice your cut. Let me look at it."

Michael didn't like to see her worry. "I'm okay, Britt really. Aren't you talking to your dad?"

Brittany moved his hair back to see the cut better. "Yeah I was but I heard Taylor call for a medic so I came to see what was going on."

Michael grabbed her hand that was moving his hair back and kissed it. "Britt, go back to your dad. I am okay. I promise."

Michael saw movement behind Brittany; he looked around and saw her dad standing in the doorway watching his and Brittany's exchange. Brittany looked over her shoulder to see what Michael was looking at. She saw her dad's face and jumped up. She left Michael's side and pushed her dad back down the hall.

The medics and Taylor came rushing in. "I'm really okay. It's just a little cut."

The medic put on his gloves and looked at his cut. "You're going to need a few stitches. I can take you to the hospital if you want."

Michael shook his head. There was no way he was leaving Brittany again, even with cops in the house. "No, I'm not leaving. If you can't do it here, then I just won't go."

The medic took out his kit. "I'll do it here but I can't give you anything to numb it, okay?"

Michael didn't care, because he didn't even feel the cut so he doubted he would feel the stitches. "That's fine. Just do it."

Twenty-nine stitches later, the medic packed up and left. Michael's head stung a little but not too bad. He got up and went to the kitchen for something to drink. Most of the cops had left by then. Brittany was still talking to her dad. Michael could hear her dad yelling and Brittany yelling back. He couldn't understand what they were saying to each other but he had a few ideas. He'd decided to go save her, but before he could reach the door it opened and her dad walked out with Brittany not far behind him. Officer Johnson looked Michael in the eyes but never said a word. He walked out the front door and didn't look back.

Brittany stood at the door looking down at her feet. "Well he knows about everything and as you can see, isn't happy about it. I didn't expect him to be. It went better than I thought though. He promised to back off of you and look into Ashley's murder more. How many stitches did you have to get?"

Michael pulled Brittany close to him and hugged her. "Twenty-nine." She looked up and moved his hair back to see the stitches. She didn't say a word and just hugged him back. Michael pulled away. "I'm going to go clean up the glass. Why don't you go pour you a glass of wine and go talk to Taylor? She's pretty shook up too." She nodded and walked off to the living room.

\*\*\*

Brittany got to the door with her dad and asked him to go to her office so they could talk. She wasn't looking forward to telling him everything and honestly didn't know where to start. She closed the door and sat at her desk chair. Her dad sat on the couch. "Brittany, you want to tell me what the hell is going on?" Brittany noticed her dad's eyes were a little red. They got like that when he was stressed about something.

She folded her hands in her lap and thought about what

to say. "I don't know where you want me to start Dad." She felt stupid for feeling like a little kid afraid of being scolded by her dad. She was an adult and could make her own decisions; her dad would just have to get over it.

"I'll start from the beginning. Michael got released from prison and reached out to me for help. I wasn't sure at the time what he wanted from me but I still agreed to talk with him to see what I could do. He told me that he didn't kill Ashley eight years ago. He proceeded to tell me that he wanted to find out who did kill her and he wanted my help. I listened to what he said and told him that I couldn't promise I would help. He told me about a note that was left at his house in his room. It simply said Ashley and Jenny on it. He was worried that whoever killed Ashley was going to come after his mom. He also told me that when he got out of prison he went to see Ashley's mother and ask her some questions. He said she answered his questions and he left."

Brittany could see her dad's emotions boiling over, so she decided to leave out the part about Michael breaking into Ashley's mother's home. Her dad stood up and started to pace. "I didn't know if I could help him with anything but I told him I would check his files from his past and see what I could find out. I got access to his files but there wasn't anything out of the ordinary in it. He did have a file that was sealed and I couldn't get into it. I called him and he came over so we could talk about what it was. We knew it had to be big for me not to be able to get into it. Anyway, someone I know is going to come over and open it in two days."

Her dad stopped pacing. "Is that all?"

Brittany shook her head. "Michael and I began to be around each other more and more, while trying to find out who the real killer was. The killer changed his mind to kill Michael's mother and wanted me dead instead. I received a package at work a few days ago. I brought it home and opened it. It had a diary in it and a note. Dad the diary was Ashley's and the note had to be from the real killer. Michael insisted on me telling you and other cops but I didn't want to. I figured we could figure it out on our own and when enough evidence came in then we could come to you about it. We put the diary and note back in the package and in my safe. Long story short Taylor is staying with me. She left to get some stuff from work and Michael went to see his mom. The killer saw I was alone and came after me. Michael showed up just in time and fought with the killer but he got away."

Brittany watched her dad for a reaction. His face gave away nothing as he sat back on the couch. "I don't get any of it, Brittany. After everything I went through to put that bastard behind bars for killing that poor girl, you're trying to tell me he didn't do it? Why the hell would you even help someone that I hate so much? None of this proves he didn't kill Ashley! What if he is just trying to make himself look innocent Brittany? You think it was just perfect timing that he showed up as the killer came to kill you? You're wrong! He tried to say that he showed up and found Ashley dead back then! So, he just happened to do that two times? I can't believe you would do this behind my back! You could have gotten killed Brittany! And for what? Some guy who has a record?"

Brittany jumped up because she had heard enough. "That's enough! I'm not a child anymore and frankly I didn't even have to tell you any of this. Look Dad, I love you very much but I am not wrong about Michael. He didn't kill Ashley and he didn't try to cover it up by having me killed. That's a low blow even for you. I didn't hide anything from you. What I do in my home is none of your business. If all you're going to do is blame Michael, then you can leave. He saved my life and you should be happy about that. I'm not even asking you to get along with him. Hell, I'm not asking anything from you, I just wanted to tell you what was going on. I can see now I shouldn't have! I understand you think he is guilty but open your damn eyes Dad! Swallow your pride and look at the facts. He didn't do any of it and you're wrong. It would be nice to have you on my side about this but I can see that won't happen. I care about Michael a lot and I am going to help him. None of this is his fault no matter how bad you want it to be." Brittany was steaming. She was so mad she had tears in her eyes.

Her dad looked at her and his whole face changed. He didn't speak for a while. He got up and walked to the wall where her plaques were hanging. "I'll consider Ashley's murder again but I won't make any promises about finding anything. I had a sharper eye back then, not so much now. I will have cops watch your house. I need any evidence that you have and I will need you to stay home from work. I will also need to see whatever is in that file once you get it opened. I won't ever like him Brittany, I didn't back then and I won't now. Don't come to me looking for approval because you won't get it from me. I love you very much but I can't be around him. I hope you understand Brittany." He walked to the door and opened it, walking out with whole new meaning to hurt showing on his face.

# CHAPTER EIGHTEEN

D*amn it! That son of a bitch walked in on me.* The mysterious man saw everyone leave and figured it was the perfect time to break in. He easily entered through the front door but was stopped by the bedroom lock. He was so close he could smell her. Michael came out of nowhere acting like a hero. The mysterious man got a few punches in on Michael but he felt he would lose the fight if he didn't run. He panicked because he couldn't go out the way he came because Michael would catch him.

He ran to the window and jumped through it. Glass went everywhere and he managed to fall on his side. He was glad he didn't break a leg being that it was the second floor of the house. He stumbled as he jumped up. Michael was close behind him but he felt that he would be able to lose him in the woods. After being in the woods a few days the mysterious man knew five to six different ways to get back to his car. He chose the path that had briers and thorn bushes hoping that would slow Michael down. His plan worked and Michael quickly became lost in the woods. Once in his car the mysterious man changed his wig and hat to avoid detection. He drove off in the direction of his hotel.

He didn't hear any sirens so he figured they truly were stupid and didn't call the cops. He knew Brittany wouldn't want her dad to know about Michael and her being together. Either way he needed to lay low and make a new plan; one that included Michael dying with Brittany. A possible murder suicide would do the trick. He hated to kill Michael but at that point what other choice did he have?

\*\*\*

Michael picked up what he could of the glass and began looking for the vacuum cleaner. He opened her closet door and something silver between her clothes caught his attention. He pushed her clothes aside to see what it was. It was a door handle. *That's weird. Why would she have a hidden door in her closet?* He pushed the handle down and the door opened. He felt for a switch. Once the light came on his jaw dropped. There were guns all along the walls. 410 shot guns, 12 gauge shot guns, pistols, and rifles of all kinds. He couldn't believe it. *Why the hell didn't she grab one of these and shoot the bastard earlier? Maybe she didn't have time to get one before he came in? Maybe she just panicked.* Either way it was the best arsenal he had ever seen. *She's more than just a tom boy. She's a hot tom boy with guns,* he thought as he cut the light off and shut the door. He tried to make the clothes look like they did and then backed out of the closet. He turned to walk downstairs to find the vacuum and ran into Brittany. She was leaning up against the door way of her room smiling. "I see you got nosy and found my collection?"

"I don't know if I would call that a collection or a preparation for the zombie apocalypse!"

She laughed as she pushed the vacuum through the doorway. She plugged it in then vacuumed the floor where glass was. He asked her if there were any more surprises. She quickly said "no" as she vacuumed. He waited until she was done vacuuming and asked, "Where does the vacuum go?"

"In Taylor's closet."

They walked down the stairs together. Michael placed

the vacuum in the closet and went to the living room where Brittany and Taylor were. They were engaged in conversation when there was a knock at the door. Everyone jumped. They were on edge for sure. Michael stood and went to see who it was. The girls poked their heads around the corner of the living room doorway peeking at the entryway. Michael looked through the peephole and sighed in relief. He opened the door and Mark walked in. "Hey man, I am so sorry I left! I didn't think anything would happen with Taylor here. I shouldn't have left but Ma fell and was hurt. I had to go help her," Mark said looking sad.

Michael felt bad for Mark. He hated seeing his best friend beat himself up over something he couldn't help. "Dude it would have happened no matter what. It isn't your fault. We are all safe. A little shook up but we are good man. If you need to go back to your mom you can, I'll understand."

Mark shook his head and said, "No, she is resting and told me to leave. Plus, my aunt is helping take care of her so I'm good to hang."

"Look Mark, it's really okay. Don't beat yourself up, dude. The guy was sitting at Brittany's house the whole time waiting for us to leave. Also, if we didn't leave he might have gotten mad and came in to hurt us all. It's not your fault or Taylor's. We got a few bumps but it's not a big deal. Britt is okay and so am I. Plus this gives us time to plan and to think of who it could be. I doubt he will be coming back anytime soon after all that. That fall he took out of the window had to hurt too," Michael said with a pat to Mark's back.

"Okay man," Mark said with a forced smile. "Is Taylor here?"

"She sure is. As a matter of fact, they are spying on us again."

They both laughed and headed to the living room. Mark

and Taylor cuddled on the floor while Michael and Brittany cuddled on the couch.

Brittany jumped up off the couch, startling Michael. "In all the fuss I forgot to give the note and diary to my dad! How the hell did I manage to forget that?" She got her phone off the table. "I have to let my dad know so they can put it into evidence! Maybe they can pull prints off it or something." She walked off to the kitchen and called her dad.

Michael, Mark, and Taylor were talking about everything that happened when Brittany rejoined them. "My dad is going to drop by tomorrow on his way to work. He's sending someone over to watch the house in case the guy comes back."

Michael nodded. He hated cops, but in that case a little extra protection wouldn't hurt. Brittany sat down with Michael. "I don't know about you guys but I'm starving. Y'all want to call in some food somewhere?"

Michael hadn't eaten all day and was starving too. "Sure, what about the sub shop in town? They don't deliver but we can all ride and get it."

They all piled into Taylor's car because it was a four door. Michael and Brittany sat in the back while Mark and Taylor were up front. They rode in silence for a while until they reached town. Michael was the one who broke the silence. "Okay, so I have to know something. We are all close friends, now right?" Everyone answered yes and looked at him funny. "Okay, so can y'all please tell me what's going on with you two?"

"Well...Well...It's um..."

Michael laughed and Brittany tried to hide her laugh as Mark stuttered on his words.

Taylor looked over at Mark and took over for him. "Well we kind of discussed that last night. We don't want just a fling but until my divorce is final we need to keep it on the low down. So, we are just going with the flow of things."

Mark nodded to agree with Taylor. "Well if it makes y'all feel any better, I think y'all are good for each other. So just in case y'all care, I approve," Brittany said as she laughed a little.

Michael grabbed Brittany's hand and held it. "I agree with Britt. I approve too!"

Taylor and Mark laughed and said, "Thank you," in unison.

When they got to the sub shop, Brittany and Taylor got out to get the food. Afterwards, they rode back to Brittany's house in silence, engulfed in the aroma of their subs.

Once at Brittany's house, Michael carried the food inside and put it on the table. He got him and Brittany a drink while Mark got his and Taylor's. They all sat at the table and ate while they chit chatted. Once done eating, everyone found their way back to the living room. Brittany asked everyone to play a game to lighten the mood. The game was called heads up like a TV show the girls watched. You stuck a card to you head with a title on it while everyone gives you hints so you can guess what the word is. Brittany was good at clue giving but not so great at guessing. Mark sucked at the game all around but they all had fun laughing at him. There were times when they had trouble breathing from laughing so hard. Michael was surprised at how fun the game really was.

Michael heard a knock on the door over the laughter. He got up and snuck off so no one would get jumpy again. Once at the door he looked through the peep hole; it was a cop. He opened the door. "What can I do for you officer?"

Michael asked as nice as he could.

"Good evening sir. I just wanted to let you know I will be keeping an eye out for the next ten to twelve hours. Someone new will come in once my shift is over."

Michael nodded and shut the door. He didn't have anything else to say to the cop. He locked the door and went back to the living room. Apparently it was his turn because they all were waiting on him. Brittany looked up at him. "Who was that?"

"It was a cop saying that he was going to keep a watch out for a while and then someone else would take over once his shift was over."

Everyone nodded and went back to the game. The adventures of the day were temporally forgotten.

***

The mysterious man knew he got hurt during the fall but it didn't really occur to him how bad until he got to his hotel room. There were a few shards of glass in his side and possibly a broken rib. He just wanted to drive over and kill them all for walking in on him. He should have used a gun and just shot Michael, but he knew the cops would look for him. He couldn't have that. No, he needed to make it look like a murder suicide because that was the only choice he had left. He pulled the glass out of his side and wrapped himself tight with some gauze around his ribs. He needed to gain some strength before attacking again. *Next time I won't fail. I'll do what I came here to do once and for all.*

***

Michael was the first one up the next morning. He showered, brushed his teeth, and even cleaned his stitches before anyone else woke up. He snuck downstairs quietly not wanting to wake anyone and made himself some coffee.

While in the kitchen, he decided to have breakfast delivered to them that morning, instead of cooking. He knew what Mark and Brittany ate but Taylor was a mystery. He decided to go with something simple and called the order in. He took his coffee and went to the back door; he wanted to get some air. He reached for the door when he heard a knock coming from the front door. He figured it had to be another cop. Annoyed he went to the door and looked out the peephole. To his surprise, it wasn't just any cop, it was Officer Johnson. *Well this is going to be good.* He opened the door and faced the man that hated him.

"Morning Johnson, what can I do for you?" Michael tried not to start an argument with him. After all he did agree to look into Ashley's case some more. Whether or not he meant it was the real question.

"Where is Brittany?"

Michael took a sip of his coffee. "She is still in bed. I was trying to let her sleep. If you want to wait for her to wake up, then feel free to come in. I made coffee if you want some." Michael opened the door to show he was willing to let him in.

"You can cut the shit, Michael. For some stupid reason Brittany is letting you in her life. Even though I don't like it, I can't make up her mind for her. However, I will never like you so let's get something straight; I don't have to and won't ever be nice to you. So you can stop pretending to like me. Also, the only reason I am here is to grab the evidence before I go to work. So, go get it so I can go."

Michael smiled. "I was only being nice for Brittany. Don't worry. My feelings about you haven't changed either and never will. You're crazy to think I would like you after putting me in prison for some shit I didn't do. I promise before it's all over you will apologize to me because you will finally see the truth. Again, I don't like you and never will. I just won't let your sour mood rub off on me or Brittany. I might act or talk like I am okay with you sir, but I'm not so don't forget it. Now if you want to wait right here that will be just fine. I'll be right back."

Michael was pleased with how he handled that. At first all he wanted to do was say a few choice words and slam the damn door in his face. He walked upstairs trying to stay quiet. He got on the floor in Brittany's room and pulled out her safe to get the package with the notes and diary. Michael had already taken pictures of everything so he would have it if he needed it. He pushed the safe back under the bed and heard Brittany sigh and roll over on her side. She was still asleep so he let her rest. He walked out of the room with the package.

Once at the front door he handed Officer Johnson the package. "My prints are only on the note I found in my room. Everything else I used gloves." Michael didn't wait for a response he just shut the door back and locked it. He didn't care for anything else Officer Johnson had to say. He went to the kitchen table and waited for the food to arrive.

# CHAPTER NINETEEN

Mark tiredly walked into the kitchen and poured himself some coffee.

"Didn't sleep good last night, bro?"

Mark smiled at Michael and joined him at the kitchen table. "I didn't sleep at all if you know what I'm saying."

Michael laughed a little and drank the rest of his coffee. "So, you have to be honest with me man. What is going on with you and Taylor? Don't forget I know you just as good as you know me."

Mark took a sip of his coffee and set it back down on the table. "I really don't know man. You know I don't keep a steady girlfriend ever. It just isn't my thing, but with Taylor it feels different. I think it's because I was always looking for a girl to fit what I wanted. The only problem was every girl had something different but not all of it in one girl. Do you remember Sam from school?"

Michael nodded. Sam was a beauty with long blond hair. She was smart and a volleyball star.

"Well I was seeing her for a while. She was pretty great. She was hot, sweet, and easy to talk to. The thing is she was missing something. All the girls in my life have been missing something, but with Taylor she has it all. I don't feel like I need to look for anyone else. Anyway, the only thing that stands in our way is her divorce. This sucks because now

I'm stuck in the same boat you are, being hidden in the dark."

Michael laughed. "It's not too bad, but if you get tired of being cooped up just take her out to the next town over. No one will know her or you there. That's what me and Brittany did and still do."

Mark's face lit up with the thought. "I will definitely have to do that soon."

Michael heard someone knock at the door. He got up and grabbed his wallet off the island and walked to the door. He paid for the food and brought it to the kitchen table. He set the food down and began to separate it. He went to grab a serving tray from the bottom cabinet. He saw them the other day when they grilled out. Michael placed a plate on the tray and took it to the table with Mark watching him like a hawk.

He placed Brittany's food on the plate with a cup of coffee and a glass of orange juice. Then he added a napkin and a fork to the tray.

"Dude does she have another tray? I want to do the same thing for Taylor," Mark asked.

"Yeah in the bottom cabinet there is another one and you know where the plates are. I got Taylor the same thing I got Britt; I didn't really know what she liked."

"She will love this. Thanks, man."

Michael got the tray and carefully took it up to Brittany's room. Once he got into the room, Brittany was out of bed and in the bathroom. He placed the food on the bed and grabbed a note pad and a pen from her nightstand. He wrote her a sweet note before he walked back downstairs and ate his food in the kitchen. Once he finished, he put his plate in the sink and checked the time. It was nine twenty. He went upstairs to see Brittany. When he walked in, she was in bed eating.

Michael walked over and sat next to Brittany. She put down her fork and looked over at him. "Good morning, handsome."

She had a way of looking at him that made his heart skip a beat. "Good morning, beautiful. I hope you like your food and no, I didn't cook it."

She laughed, picking up her fork and moving her eggs around with her fork. "I could tell you didn't. The pancakes don't taste like yours, but I still like them. Thank you for doing all this and letting me get some sleep."

He reached over and placed his hand on her leg. He was happy he could make her smile. He planned to be doing that for a long time.

"How is the head wound?"

Michael looked away. "I can't really tell it's even there. I'll take the stitches out in a few days and it will be fine." He could tell Brittany didn't like the idea of that but she didn't push the issue.

***

Brittany still couldn't believe how sweet Michael was. He showed her everyday how much he loved her. She finished eating her breakfast and went to take her tray downstairs when Michael stopped her. "I'll take that downstairs. I want us to have a lazy day or at least a lazy morning. I'll be right back. Don't move."

She didn't argue with him, mainly because he was gone with her tray before she could. She needed to go down and talk to Taylor. Maybe he wouldn't be upset if she just ran down really quick and talked to her. Brittany got up off the bed and headed for the door. Michael made it back to the door before she could escape. "I was uh...I was going to ask Taylor something."

"Well you can ask her in a little bit, besides she is having breakfast in bed."

Brittany turned around and got back in bed; which wasn't easy for her. She never stayed in bed long and the thought was driving her crazy. At least Michael was there to keep her entertained. He grabbed her hand. "So, what do you want to do today?" Brittany had no clue. Could she even leave her house with some crazy person out there after her? She wasn't sure but maybe she and Taylor could come up with something to do for the guys.

"I might have something I need to do today but I have to talk to Taylor first." She smiled and tried to hide the fact that she was keeping something from him.

"Okay, well for now let's just lay here and hold each other."

They both laid down, and she suddenly realized just how tired she was. She didn't know if it was because her room was dark from the curtains being closed, her mind was exhausted from everything that was going on, or the fact that Michael was holding her rubbing her head, but before she knew it she fell back asleep.

*** 

The mysterious man woke up sweating and with a fever. He looked around and remembered he was still in the shit hole of a hotel. Last he remembered was sitting down to rest the night before and apparently ended up falling asleep. His ribs were killing him from the jump out the window. He looked at the clock to see the time. *Damn! It's eleven o'clock*. He had to get up. He had shit to get done. He knew Michael and Brittany had to be on edge ever since his attack.

He also knew that he needed to lay low for a little while and keep his distance, but being away kept him from knowing what they were doing and he didn't like it.

He got up off the bed slowly, wincing as he stood up. He grabbed his bag and placed it on the bed. He searched the bag of goodies for his GPS devices. *Shit, there were four cars,* he thought when he found two GPSs. He sifted through the wigs, rope, duct tape, gloves, and hats hoping to find more. Unfortunately, he had only brought two with him. He sat down on the bed trying to think of a plan. *I can put one on each girl's cars. That way if all four of them went somewhere they would end up taking the four-door car and if Michael went anywhere he would more than likely take that bitch's car.* The mysterious man walked over to the table and opened up his laptop. He linked the GPSs to the laptop to make sure they worked right before he got a knife to scratch the serial numbers off of the devices.

Once he was satisfied with the GPSs, he tended to his wound. He got some rags and rubbing alcohol out of his bag. As he undid the wrap on his ribs, he saw bruising along with the fact that his cuts were still bleeding. He poured alcohol on some rags and placed it on his cuts. He gritted his teeth to keep from yelling out; after the first few cuts the pain became bearable. He went to the bathroom to get a better look at the cuts. Most of them were small but there were two pretty good sized ones that needed stitches. *Damn it,* he thought realizing he didn't bring anything to stitch himself up. He'd have to go out and get some supplies from town. Until then, he wrapped it with new gauze and put on a shirt. He shook his head at the wounds. He still couldn't believe Michael almost caught him. *That bastard will pay soon, really soon. I'll put the GPSs on the cars tonight and watch them for a few days. Then I'll make sure he watches me kill his little bitch. Then, I'll kill his ass.*

\*\*\*

Brittany woke up and looked at the clock. It was twelve-thirty. *Oh, shit! Why did I sleep so long today?* She jumped up and went downstairs. Everyone was in the living room watching TV. She walked in and sat beside Michael on the couch.

"Well hello, sleepy head," Michael said as he kissed her and wrapped his arm around her. "I hope you got some sleep finally."

"I did, thank you." She looked over at Taylor who was on her laptop. "Hey, do you want to go do some work in my office? I have a few things I need to get done today."

"Yeah sure, all my stuff is in there anyway. You have a fax machine, right?" Brittany nodded. "Good. I have the numbers you needed yesterday, so we can send everything we need to from here. I also got the files you wanted yesterday and forwarded all the calls to my cell phone. I would have done it to your phone but I would rather mine blow up then yours."

Brittany got up off the couch and followed Taylor into the office. Taylor sat on the couch, and got out all the papers Brittany needed while Brittany sat at her desk. She took the files from Taylor and placed them in front of her. They worked for the next two hours on getting papers sent out to everyone they needed to. Brittany forgot how much work could take your mind off of things. Taylor seemed more relaxed then too. Brittany decided to take a break and talk to Taylor about Michael. She needed Taylor's help with figuring out something to do for Michael because she was drawing blanks with ideas.

"So, Taylor I need some help with something. Michael has been doing a ton of stuff for me, including saving my life. I want to do something for him but I don't know what to do. At first I was going to buy him something, but I can't leave the house without him. Then I figured I would buy something online and have it sent here but he would be the one to open the door and get the package. I'm drawing blanks here and I need help!"

Taylor looked up from her computer and smiled at Brittany. "That's really sweet. I'm not sure what you could do though. I would say make him dinner but he'd find a way of helping you do that."

Brittany got up and paced the floor in thought. Taylor put her computer on the table and jumped up and exclaimed, "I've got an idea!"

Brittany put her finger up to her mouth. "Shhhh. He might hear you!"

Taylor sat back down and mouthed "*sorry*".

Brittany laughed and sat back at her desk. "Okay, so what's your idea?"

"So, my parents have a summer house in North Carolina that they aren't using right now. It's a big three bedroom cabin in the woods. It would be perfect. It has a hot tub, a private pool, and even a pool table in it. We could get away and relax for a few days. It would do us some good. The killer won't find us there so we could go hide out for a while. Plus, the cops could watch your house so if he does come here then they could catch him. I'm sure Michael will love it there."

Brittany sat silent for a minute. Would it be okay to leave for a few days? She knew the killer wouldn't be back for a while because of the cops; Taylor was right about that. The big question was would Michael want to go? She was a little worried he wouldn't want to go because of everything that was going on. "That would be great, Taylor. Here is what we do. You pack your clothes and I'll pack mine. Try to do it where they won't know okay? Then we will just tell the guys that we need to go to town. While we are in town we will go by Marks house and tell him to get some clothes for a trip. We will go by Michael's house and get some clothes for him too, but we won't tell them where we are going, okay?"

Taylor smiled and then looked down at her feet. "I have a speed bump in our plan; Mark's job. I know he said he has some vacation time stacked up because we were talking about going to the next town over for a night. I just don't know how we could get him to take it off without telling him what's going on."

"Wait a minute. Do you know where he works?"

"Why?" Taylor asked as she nodded her head.

"Maybe we can call and explain things to his boss and see if they'll put it in for him. Google the name of the place and get the number so I can call."

Taylor went to work on the computer until she finally found it. She read off the number to Brittany.

"Okay Taylor, open the door and see where the guys are. We can't let them hear me."

Taylor cracked the door and poked her head out. She shut the door back and smiled at Brittany. "They are on the back porch. This is perfect, make the call."

The receptionists answered the phone. "Hello this is Wades Delivery Service, how can I direct your call?"

"Yes, I am trying to reach someone in the HR department please. This is Brittany Johnson."

"Oh, okay Ms. Johnson please hold and I will transfer you."

Brittany had a feeling the lady knew her. She was the

only lawyer in town so her name was pretty big to people. Another lady answered the phone. "This is Tabitha speaking how can I help you Ms. Johnson?"

"Hello Tabitha. I have a quick question for you. I am planning a trip tomorrow with someone who works for you. The problem is that it's a surprise and I don't want him to know about it. I know legally I can't put in vacation for him but I wanted to know if he calls tomorrow and puts it in would it get approved."

"Well who is it we are talking about Ms. Johnson, so I can pull up his file to make sure he has vacation time to put in?"

"His name is Mark Summers."

"Mark, let me see. Oh yes, he has plenty of time to take off. I normally make them put it in at least two weeks in advance though. You said you're leaving tomorrow?"

"Yes, we are leaving tomorrow. I know its short notice but the availability for our place we are staying at just became open. We have been on the list for a while and if we don't take it now then we might not get another chance. If there was more time I assure you I would have followed the rules."

Brittany looked over at Taylor who was biting her nails and shaking her leg.

"Well okay Ms. Johnson just this one time. How many days do you think he will need?"

Taylor and Brittany hadn't discussed the days so Brittany went with what she felt was the best time period. "I am thinking a week would do. I have the place booked for eight days but we can come back in seven, if that's okay."

"Yes, that's fine. I'll write it down in his file. He will just need to call tomorrow and confirm it so I can put it in for him."

"Thank you."

"You're welcome. Remember to have him call me tomorrow to confirm it or else it won't get put in okay?"

Brittany agreed with the woman and hung up the phone.

"Well?" Taylor asked on pins and needles.

"He is off for a week. I figured he could use the time off even if we weren't at the cabin."

Taylor ran over and hugged Brittany then sat back down. "Okay, so how the hell do we pack without them knowing? Mark is up my butt in this house and so is Michael with you."

*Taylor is right.* "Hmmmmm...What could we give them to do that would distract them for a while?"

"Does Michael like to target practice? Mark loves it and you do have an army in your closet," Taylor said with a chuckle.

"He would like that. I'll even tell the cops that are on watch that it's me firing the guns off so they won't bother them. It should give us a while; I do have a ton of guns plus I'll make them clean the guns once they are done. I could help you pack as long as you help me too."

Brittany got up and Taylor followed her. They opened the back door and walked onto the deck. Mark and Michael were sitting at the table and each had a beer. "What are y'all up to out here?" Brittany asked.

"We were just keeping an eye out. Are y'all done working?"

Brittany shook her head. "No, just taking a break. I do

have a question though."

Michael looked at her curiously.

"Me and Taylor have a lot of work to get done. I know we can't leave the house because of psycho, and I know y'all have to be bored. By any chance would y'all mind shooting some of my guns and cleaning them. I try to do it once a month but I haven't had time to. I have enough ammo and plenty of targets too."

Michael and Mark's eyes got huge.

Mark jumped up and said, "Wait! How many guns do you have and if it's a lot can we shoot any one of them we want?"

Brittany had to think about how many she had. She looked at it sort of like an investment to herself. She always knew if she ever needed money she could just sell a gun and be okay. "I think I have forty-two, but I'm not sure. And yes you can shoot whatever you want."

Mark's mouth dropped open and his eyes looked like they were going to pop out of his head. Michael had already gotten up to go inside. The girls followed them upstairs to Brittany's room. Brittany made her way around the guys and went to the closet. She pushed the clothes aside and opened the hidden door. Mark was right behind her.

"Holy shit, you have a secret room for your guns?"

Brittany giggled and flipped the light switch. "Yes, I do. Okay, so take what you want outside to the table and don't worry if you can't remember where to put them back at. I have the shelves labeled so I can show you if you forget. The ammo is on the same shelf that the gun is on and I have extra in the safe in the corner over there."

Mark stepped into the room. "Dude, I am coming here

for the zombie apocalypse!"

Brittany could only laugh at him. Michael walked over and got her favorite gun down. It was her grandfather's 30-06 rifle with a dark brown wood stock. She'd never missed a deer with that one. She decided to leave them to picking out their guns.

"Okay, y'all have fun and please just clean them."

Brittany went to her side of the bed to grab her phone when she hit her toe on the safe. *That's weird. Why is the safe sticking out?* She opened the safe and started to panic. *Where is the package with all the stuff in it?*

"Michael!"

Michael ran into the room with guns in his arms. "What's wrong?"

"Did you take the stuff out of the safe?"

He put the guns on the bed. "Oh, I forgot to tell you that your dad came by this morning and asked for it all so I gave it to him. I didn't want to wake you. I'm sorry. I just forgot to tell you he came by."

"That's fine. I just panicked when I didn't see it in here. Was my dad an ass to you?"

Michael only smiled, picked up the guns, and followed Mark downstairs. Brittany took that as a yes. Pushing the safe under her bed she got her phone and went down to Taylor's room to pack.

# CHAPTER TWENTY

Michael and Mark were out shooting the guns while the cop that was on guard watched. When Brittany told him that they were going to be shooting off guns he wanted to join in and Brittany didn't mind. While the guys played with the guns, Brittany and Taylor each packed a bag of clothes. Brittany grabbed a small luggage bag for her and Taylor to share; they placed their makeup and bathroom items in it. She was careful not to pack a lot of toiletries, afraid that Michael might notice if too many things were missing. She made a mental note to grab the rest of her things and Michael's soap before they left. Once they were done, she and Taylor put their luggage in Taylor's closet so the guys wouldn't find it.

Taylor went and took a shower while Brittany went to the backyard. She was happy to see that the guys found her earmuffs in the closet. She grabbed a set of earmuffs, picked up one of the guns, and joined them. Michael turned around to see Brittany standing there with the gun. He took his earmuffs off and walked up to her. "You look sexy all the time but there is something about you holding that gun that just does it to me." Brittany smiled and waited for Mark to put down his gun. Once he did, she walked past the cop and Michael. She loaded the gun with the bullet in her pocket, took the safety off, aimed, and fired. Just like always, she hit the target right in the center. She put another bullet in and put off another shot and another shot. After putting the safety back on, she walked back to where she was standing.

Michael never took his eyes off of her. She laughed at the way he looked at her.

"I haven't met anyone who can shoot this gun like me. As a matter of fact, if this officer doesn't mind I'd like to place a bet with you all." Everyone including the cop nodded. "I bet I can shoot three shots into the center of that target and y'all won't get one in. I'll even put a hundred dollars on it."

Michael looked confused at first. "Okay, so what's the catch? Is there something wrong with the gun? Does it shoot a little off and you just know the right place to aim to get it right?"

"No, I promise the gun is perfectly sighted in. I just never met anyone who can do it three times in a row like I can."

Michael put his earmuffs back on and took the gun from her. "Okay, sweet cheeks, you're on."

Brittany smiled and handed him the bullets. Brittany watched Michael load the gun and shoot. Brittany smirked because she could tell he didn't hit the center.

"Damn it! Okay, so I'm out."

The cop laughed and took the gun from Michael. "I'm not betting but I want to give it a shot." Brittany just nodded and waited. The cop took the shot and sure enough he missed the center. However, he got closer than Michael did.

"My turn!" Mark said as he got the gun and aimed at the target. He missed it to.

"Okay Britt so what's the big deal?"

Brittany laughed. "I honestly don't know. No one I know has ever been able to hit the center with this gun except me.

Here give me another gun that you can hit the center with and I'll show you it's sighted right." Michael handed her another rifle. Putting the bullet in and taking off the safety she aimed and fired. Sure, enough she hit the center of the target. "Well boys, I've had enough showing off for one day I'm going in. Don't forget to clean them before you put them up, okay?" All the guys mumbled and went back to shooting.

After the guys got done shooting, everyone ate lunch and hung out in the living room. Brittany and Taylor had a hard time the rest of the day not saying anything about the trip. Every once in a while she would catch Taylor looking at her and they would both just smile. They spent the rest of their evening playing a few board games and hanging out. Around seven o'clock Brittany started to get hungry. "Hey what do y'all want to eat for dinner?"

Everyone just looked at her for a second. Michael finally spoke up, "We bought some stuff to make homemade pizza. There is also stuff to make burgers in there too. I'm good with either."

Brittany liked the sound of pizza. "Pizza it is! This time I'm cooking it alone. Y'all can relax." Everyone just nodded. Brittany got up and walked out of the living room.

Taylor followed behind her. "Don't worry I won't help. I just want to keep you company."

Brittany especially was excited about getting away. She started making the dough and whispering to Taylor. "Do you think they have any idea?"

"I don't think they have any clue and I don't know how or why they would. We have been quiet about this whole thing." Brittany nodded and put the dough in a bowl. Then she went to the sink to wash the flour and dough off her hands.

Brittany happily prepared dinner as she and Taylor talked. After the pizza was finished they all sat at the table and ate. Everyone commented on how great her pizza was. That made Brittany happy because she got the recipe out of her mom's old cook book. It was one of the few things Brittany kept after her mom passed away.

Michael and Mark agreed to clean up since Brittany cooked. Brittany didn't mind it and they seemed happy to do it. Brittany and Taylor sat down in the living room while Mark and Michael cleaned. It was weird to have so many people in her house. She'd gotten used to being alone for a long time, and now she had three other people living with her; well two and a tag along. She laughed at the thought that Mark was Michael's best friend and was now Taylor's lover. It was a weird circle of friends but she loved every second of their company.

Brittany knew she had to make sure she went to bed early so she could awake before Michael. He always found a way to wake up before she did, but she had to get the car packed. "We have to wake up before the guys do so we can get our stuff in the car."

Taylor nodded and looked off in the distance, "Wait Britt, why don't we agree on a time tonight and put it in the car while they are asleep? That way if they get up before us we won't have to worry about it."

Brittany liked that plan a lot better. "Okay, that will work. Let's plan on meeting in the living room at three in the morning. Then after my friend comes by to open the file, we can say we need to go get something from my office and get some food. They will go with us and our plan will be in motion." Brittany was a little worried about what the news in the file would be. She hoped it wouldn't be something to ruin their trip. Knowing the guys would be back in the living room in any minute, they changed the subject.

The rest of the night went just like normal. They watched a movie and everyone went off to bed. Brittany and Michael once again showered together, with her still not allowing him to see her stomach. When they got into bed Brittany stared at Michael and said, "I really do love you." He kissed her and she could feel how much he loved her. Without words, Michael spent the next hour showing her just how much he loved her.

At three o'clock her phone vibrated and woke Brittany up. She rolled over trying to make sure not to wake Michael. He was softly snoring and seemed to be good and asleep. She inched her way out of her room and down the dark stairs; hoping she wouldn't trip and fall down all the stairs. She made it all the way into the living room and saw Taylor sitting on the couch. "Did you get our bags?" she whispered. Taylor didn't say anything. "If you're nodding Taylor I can't see you."

"Oh sorry," she whispered back. "Yes, I got both our bags."

Brittany headed to the front door with the bags while Taylor got her keys off the island. They met at the door and carefully eased out. Once outside they put the bags in the trunk of Taylor's car and closed it quietly. There was always something about the dark that didn't sit well with Brittany. She didn't know what it was but she always felt like someone was watching her. With the ordeal with the killer fresh in her brain the feeling was worse. Taylor and Brittany hurried back into the house and locked the door. Without a word to each other, both of them went back to bed. Once Brittany made it back into bed Michael woke up. "Where did you go, babe?" Brittany froze. *Oh shit, does he know I went outside? No, he couldn't. We were quick and quiet.*

"I went to get something to drink."

"Oh," he said as he pulled her close to him.

Michael fell right back to sleep but Brittany couldn't. She still had a feeling like someone was watching her. She didn't know if it was her mind or the fact that she was almost attacked by a psycho. Either way it took her a while to fall asleep.

\*\*\*

*They grew enough balls to call the cops*, the mysterious man thought when he saw the cop camped alongside the road. It didn't bother him at all. It was dark and where the cop car was parked at he wouldn't get caught going up to their cars. Just as he was about to move from his position, the front door opened. The mysterious man watched Brittany and Taylor come outside with bags and put them in the trunk. At that moment, he was glad he brought the tracking devices. Brittany kept looking in his direction while she was outside. He knew she couldn't see him or hear him but it was almost like she saw right through him. Once she closed the trunk, they ran back inside. It was his chance to put the devices on the cars. He quietly moved to the car and slid under it. He winced a little while he put the GPS tracker on the car. His ribs were killing him but it needed to be done. It was obvious that they were planning to leave soon and he needed to be ready to follow them. After he put one on each of the girl's cars he snuck back into the woods and headed for his car. He needed to get back and pack up, because it was apparent that he would be leaving town soon.

\*\*\*

Brittany woke up alone with Michael gone again. She was thankful that she and Taylor had placed the luggage in the car earlier that morning. She got dressed and headed down the stairs. She found Michael in the kitchen making coffee.

"Good morning, baby. Christine said the guy would be here sometime before noon. I'm going to go get my laptop and put it in the living room so when he gets here we can all be around to hear what's going on, unless you want to be alone with him? I mean it is your file and it could be something private."

Michael shook his head and walked closer to her. "No, you are in my life now and I won't hide anything from you. This is as much a part of you as it is me. Plus, this could be something that we all need to hear."

Brittany kissed him and stopped before walking away. "Oh, and after he leaves, me and Taylor need to go to the office and get some stuff."

Michael poured him some coffee. "Me and Mark will ride along with y'all. Plus, we can grab some food while we are out."

Brittany tried to hide a smile. Everything was going as planned and she was happy. She grabbed her lap top out of her office and went to the living room. Brittany sat on the couch and pulled up Michael's file. She had no idea what was about to be opened but she could feel it in her bones it wasn't going to be good.

# CHAPTER TWENTY-ONE

It was around ten-fifteen when there was a knock at the door. Figuring it was the man to open his file, Michael got up and went to the door. He was nervous to know what in his life was "sealed", but was ready for it all to be over. Michael got to the door and looked out the peephole. The cop stood there with a short guy with glasses and dark black hair. The guy had a nice suit on and a laptop bag over his shoulder. Michael opened the door and the cop nodded at Michael. The guy looked up at Michael. "You must be Michael. I'm William Rizzo. Brittany is expecting me."

Michael let him in as the cop moved off the porch. "Nice to meet you. We were in the living room awaiting your arrival." Michael almost laughed at how formal he sounded. Being formal just wasn't his thing.

Once in the living room, Michael introduced William to everyone. After shaking everyone's hand, William sat down on the couch. Brittany handed him her laptop and he went to work typing. Brittany sat on the couch on one side of William and Michael sat on the other. Michael tried not to look over William's shoulder but his nerves were inching him closer to him. Brittany and William were talking technology as he typed away. Michael couldn't understand any of what they were saying. Technology wasn't his thing either. A few minutes later, William sat back on the couch sighing. Michael looked at the computer, the screen was going crazy and words were moving all over the screen all on their own.

"What's going on now?" Michael asked.

William sat back up and said, "Right now the computer is opening up your file. It might take a few minutes but eventually it will open and your file will no longer be sealed. So, if you don't want this opened then say so now."

Michael couldn't say for sure if it was something he wanted open or not. He had no idea what was even in the damn file. "No, let it open it. I have to know what it is." William only nodded while Michael and Brittany watched the screen.

The computer pinged and William stood up. "My job is done. Your file is now open. Brittany, I'm sure you know how to do the rest. Please, if you have any questions feel free to call me. I am in town until later today." He handed his card to Brittany and Taylor walked him to the front door.

Brittany looked up at Michael and scooted next to him. "Are you ready for this?" Michael could only nod. Brittany began to hit a few keys and showcased what was on the file.

**Michael P. Sims 1995: File sealed. To be opened only by authorized personal.**

**Year in question 1995: James Beckon was killed and pronounced dead on January 25, 1995. Cause of death: head trauma.**

**Year in question 1995: Found near the body was a small boy five years of age. At the time, he seemed to be scared and lost. Upon further exam, he had memory loss and no idea of the events that occurred. Also a few bruises and cuts were taken care of on his body.**

**Year in question 1995: Upon searching missing child's reports, the child was identified as possibly being Michael P. Sims. Mother in question: Jenny S. Sims. Father in question: Carol A. Sims. Mother in question, reported son in question**

missing after going with father in question.

Year in question 1995: Further inspection of the crime scene where James Beckon was found dead showed signs of the father in question, Carol A. Sims, being present at the scene of the crime. There were obvious signs of a struggle next to the cliff at the scene. Further evidence concluded that the father in question, Carol A. Sims, died at the bottom of the cliff.

Year in question 1995: The body of father in question, Carol A. Sims, was never discovered. Being it was weeks before search teams could search the bottom of the cliff due to rough terrains, investigators believed the body to be missing due to wild life. Clothes and shoes that belonged to the father in question, Carol A. Sims, were found at the bottom of the cliff. Carol A. Sims was pronounced dead on January 25, 1995 along with James Beckon.

Year in question 1995: Upon further question over the weeks, Michael P. Sims still has no memory of the events from the weeks before. More questioning to the mother, Jenny S. Sims, confirms that James Beckon was a close friend of the father, Carol A. Sims. The mother, Jenny S. Sims, was questioned about the events on the day of January 25, 1995. The mother, Jenny S. Sims, stated the father, Carol A. Sims, and son, Michael P. Sims, went to meet James Beckon for no obvious serious reasons. The mother doesn't seem to know much about the dealings between James Beckon and Carol A. Sims.

Year in question 1995: Due to memory loss from Michael P. Sims the investigation was closed and not to be opened due to all evidence pointing to the deaths.

Michael didn't understand; that wasn't at all what he expected to find in his file. Then again what did he expect to find? His mother had been lying to him for years and it hurt. All his mother ever told him was that his dad ran off when he was five. *Why wouldn't she just tell me he died?* It didn't make any sense to him. So many things were going through his mind. Michael didn't have a clue what to even say so he sat silent as Brittany looked over at him.

"Wow. That's a lot to process. Are you alright? Do you still have no memory of that day Michael?"

Sadly, Michael looked into Brittany's eyes. He didn't remember anything about his dad and it always bugged him. He'd had few flash backs in his dreams years ago about cops putting him in a cop car but other than that he couldn't remember anything. "No, just a few dreams about cops but I thought it was just bad dreams."

Brittany slid closer to him holding his hand. "It's going to be okay." Michael knew what she was saying was true. It didn't affect him as much as he thought it would. The main part that got to him was his mother lying and his memory of that day being gone. "You might have witnessed a murder Michael and been in such shock that you lost your memory. It has happened in children before." Brittany rubbed the top of his hand to comfort him.

"I guess so, but who murdered whom and why?" That file had nothing to do with who was trying to frame him at all. It was like a dead end or a can of worms opened for no reason at all. It just added to his problems, not helped them. No one said a word for what felt like hours to Michael. Brittany got up and went to the kitchen with Taylor following after her.

Mark turned and looked at Michael. "I don't know bro, but it sounds like your dad murdered his friend and might have fallen off the cliff. Maybe they'd gotten into a fight or maybe everything was an accident. The bad thing is that you might never really know. Don't beat yourself up about it though." Michael could only nod his head at that moment.

Brittany came back in and folded up her laptop. "I know it's bad timing but me and Taylor need to run to the office. Maybe a ride into town will clear your head a little?"

"That sounds good to me. I don't want to sit around worrying about nothing. The past is the past for a reason, right?"

Brittany smiled at him then grabbed his hand. Taylor and Mark were the first ones out the door and Michael and Brittany followed behind. Brittany set her laptop bag down outside the door so she could lock the door behind her with her key. She picked up the bag and headed for the car. Michael wondered why she was bringing her laptop. Then figured she needed it while she was in the office. He climbed in the back seat with Mark while Taylor drove and Brittany rode in the passenger seat.

Michael stared out of the window lost in his thoughts as they headed towards town. His head started to hurt. He didn't know if it was from the stitches or if his brain was just overwhelmed with information. Taylor slowed down and Michael looked up to see where she was turning. He glanced over at Mark and he had the same look of confusion on his face. Michael tapped Brittany on the shoulder.

"Um, y'all know town is the other way, right?"

Brittany smiled at him. "We know which way town is. We were actually trying to go to your house first babe. If Mark's house is closer, we can stop there first just show us the way."

Michael was lost. "Okay, tell us what's going on. Why do we need to go to my house or Mark's house?" He looked over at Mark. "Do you know what's going on?" Mark just shook his head and looked at Taylor.

Taylor spoke, "We are taking y'all somewhere and we

need y'all to grab some clothes to stay for a while. We wanted to get out of the house for a few days. Before you even ask, no we aren't telling you where we are going."

Mark looked at Michael with his jaw hanging open. "Wait, I can't just leave. I have to work."

Brittany turned around in her seat to face him. "We called your work and spoke to the lady in HR. She said you are good to take off of work for a week. All you need to do is call in today and confirm it with her and you're good to go."

Michael was shocked that Brittany and Taylor took the time to plan everything. "Well, aren't y'all sneaky women. Just how long have y'all been planning this? Damn. You passed the road. Turn around and take that road and Mark's house is about three miles down on the right," he added to Taylor.

Brittany looked at Taylor and then back to Michael. "Well I have been wanting to do something nice for you for a while now, but with a psycho on the lose it made it hard to think of anything to do that would surprise you. So, Taylor and I came up with the plan for a trip. It's not far away but it will at least get us out of the house for a few days." Michael leaned in and kissed her. He couldn't believe she would do something so nice for him. She was really one in a million. He sat back and waited for them to get to Mark's house.

After Mark got his clothes from his house, he called his job to confirm his time off. They drove straight to Michael's mom's house. He hoped she wasn't home because he didn't really feel like talking to her about everything right then. They turned on his street and Michael began to worry. Could he really just walk in and not ask his mom about everything. He didn't think he could. They pulled up to his house and sure enough she was home. "I might take a second because I want to ask my mom some questions. I'll try to be quick." He got out of the car and went to the door. He waited a minute before going in. He didn't want to startle her or upset her so he gained as much calmness as he could and went in. His mom was on the couch watching the *Price Is Right*. She looked up at him and smiled. He tried his hardest to smile back at her but he was still hurt about her lying to him for so many years.

"Me and some friends are going out of town for a little while. Things have been crazy and we all just need some time away."

She got up off the couch and stood closer to him. "What's wrong Michael? I can always tell when something is wrong. Don't lie to me, either." Michael sighed and went to the couch. She followed him and sat next to him.

"Mom look, the other day someone broke into Brittany's house and tried to kill her. I got there just in time and the killer got away. I'm okay, I just had to have some stitches in my head but other than that we are all okay. We will be gone for a few days and I need to grab some clothes." He looked down at his feet. "Mom I need to ask you something and you have to be honest with me." Looking up at her he could tell she was serious now, she only nodded. "I had a scaled file in my name. It took just about an army to get it open but we finally did. Long story short. Why did you lie to me about my dad?"

Tears fell from his mother's eye and Michael hugged her. "Michael, I didn't want you to have flash backs of that day. You were so scared and had nightmares for months after that. You had to have witnessed something awful that day because it affected you for a long time. I was always afraid that if I brought it up you would go back to that state of mind again." She looked away and began telling her side of the story.

"Your father wasn't a nice man at all. He would cuss at

me and hit me from time to time. I grew to hate that man so much. I felt for so long that he died because of me. I prayed for God to make him go away, I just didn't know he would die. I felt like I was to blame for what happened to him. He might have been an awful man but no one deserved to die. Anyway, he offered to take you with him to go meet James. I didn't argue because his violence was only directed to me and not you. When y'all left, I had no clue I would end up calling the cops and having a search party out to find you two. When I got the call that they found you safe I broke down and told myself I was an idiot for letting you go with him that day. The investigators tried to talk to you but you had no memory of what happened. James was found dead and the cops said someone beat him to death in the head with what they thought at the time was a rock. They never found your father's body but they ruled him dead, saying he fell off the cliff."

Michael wasn't mad at his mother anymore. She did it to protect him and he saw that. He hugged her tight and whispered in her ear. "I'm not mad at you, Mom. You did the right thing. It's all in the past and there is no reason to worry about it now okay?"

She sat back on the couch and looked at him. "I don't like that someone is after you or the people you care about. Please be safe because I don't want to lose you again. I couldn't bear it."

He got up off the couch and headed to his room to pack his bag. Once his clothes were in the bag, he kissed his mother on the cheek and promised to be safe. He walked out the front door feeling a little better than he did when he went in. He got in the car and no one said a word to him. They rode in silence for a long time until they stopped for gas. He was looking forward to getting away more than ever. He needed to clear his mind and get away from all of the craziness.

# CHAPTER TWENTY-TWO

Brittany could tell Michael was hurt when he got back into the car. She decided to leave him alone with his thoughts for a little while. When she got stressed it helped when she was able to think freely. Every time she thought about his file, she had visions of a little Michael in the woods all alone next to a dead body. The things he'd seen had to been traumatic. Brittany was somewhat glad he couldn't remember because he didn't need memories like that floating in his mind. She was a little sad for him too though because she had no idea how it must have felt to have such a blank space in his mind and not be able to see it. She hurt for him and wished she could cuddle up to him and comfort him right then; but when they got to the cabin she planned to do just that.

The radio was the only noise in the car for the most part of their journey. After stopping for gas, Taylor turned on a dirt road towards the house. Brittany got excited when the woods finally displayed the house. It was so beautiful that it looked like it came out of the pages of a book. She loved her cozy little cabin home but Taylor's parents' cabin home was a mansion compared to hers. She smiled as she thought, *these few days are going to be memories well-made.*

\*\*\*

The mysterious man watched the GPS on his computer

ping at every cellular tower. They were heading south to North Carolina. He just couldn't figure out why. *Did they really think they could outsmart me and run away? Fools!* He watched the red dot travel for over an hour. He couldn't take his eyes off the screen; it was like he was in a trance. His bags were packed and ready to go. He just wanted to see where they stopped first. He wasn't in too big of a rush because he needed to get to wherever they were and find a place to stay close by. Then he would have to scope out the area to see how he could get in and out.

He crossed his fingers that they were staying at a hotel where ever they were going. If that was the case, he could just stay at the same hotel and easily break in to kill them. He watched as the dot began to travel out of the city towards the countryside. He slammed his fist on the table. "Damn it!" That was not what he wanted them to do at all. The dot stopped moving and he waited to see if it started back up. There wasn't anything around the road they were on for miles and the road looked to be a dead end too. He zoomed in on the road name and switched over to the internet. He typed in the road name and looked up the street view on the map. It was a huge house in the woods. *This is even better than the hotel. The idiots don't know how bad they messed up.* There wasn't any house on the map for miles so he had a pretty good idea that he could hide out and not be seen at all. He closed his laptop, put it in his bag, and headed for the door. The next stop would be in North Carolina to a local hotel. *Soon all this shit will be in my past once and for all.*

\*\*\*

Michael was in awe when he and the gang got out of the car. He couldn't look away from the house. It was a lot like Brittany's house just a much bigger version. "This is nice," he whispered as he looked at the picture perfect two story house with the wraparound porch. He looked over at

Brittany who seemed just as in awe as him. Taylor was at the back of the car getting the luggage. Michael walked around to help her with it.

"You seem to be familiar with this place, is it yours?"

Taylor looked up and laughed. "No, I wish. It's my parents' summer home, but I can use it whenever. They weren't using it right now so I told my mom we were coming. She had her maid stock the house with everything we will need."

Michael thought he heard her wrong at first. *A maid? What the hell do her parents do for a living?* He made a mental note to ask her later, but right then he needed to get the luggage in and check out the house.

Michael and Mark grabbed the luggage and followed the ladies into the house. They sat the luggage down inside, just past the front door. Michael couldn't believe what he was seeing. He felt like he was in a movie. *Damn. I wonder what Taylor's parents' other home looks like.* The house had tall ceilings in it that made him feel extremely small. There was a spiral staircase that went to the next floor up and apparently to a bottom floor. He figured the house was probably on a hill and the bottom floor was hidden, or it could have been a basement. He looked around the room some more and found big pictures of art all over the place. He had no idea what the abstract paintings were of but they were beautiful. There was a doorway on each side of the stairs. Behind the stairs was what he guessed was the living room.

Taylor turned and looked at everyone. "Well, welcome to my parent's summer home. If you want to follow me, I'll show y'all around." Taylor turned and walked to the doorway that was on the right side of the stairs. Everyone else followed her. It opened to a big open bedroom with French doors that went onto the porch. There was a big bed, dresser, and even a couch in the room. There was also a small fire place with a TV hanging over it. The room was painted a light brown and had pictures on the wall like in the front room. The room had a warm comforting feeling to it.

"This is one of the three bedrooms in the house. This room has a bathroom attached to it and a door to walk out onto the deck. The deck goes all the way around the house and ends up leading to some stairs where there is an in ground pool. Also on the back side of the deck there is a hot tub." Taylor walked into a doorway that led into a bathroom. The bathroom was just as big as the bedroom. There was a big bathtub with jets in it, a stand up or sit down shower with sprayers on the walls, and two sinks with some lights along the top that lit up the whole bathroom. Taylor walked them back out to the front room where the spiral stairs were.

"That room over there is just a huge dining room. If you want, I'll show you?" No one said a word and only nodded. Michael figured that everyone was as speechless as him right then. They walked in the room and it opened to a huge table with a lot of chairs. It looked like a table that family would eat at for Christmas dinner or something. There wasn't much art in there but there were cabinets with fine china in them. Taylor led them back to the front room. "Okay so now I'm going to show you the living room and kitchen. The living room is my favorite room because the windows overlook the property."

Michael followed Taylor into the living room. He walked in the big room and was taken aback. It was the best room in the house up to that point. The window went from one side of the room to the other, all the way to the kitchen, and continued into the kitchen showcasing an amazing view. There were mountains and fields for miles. He walked a little closer to get a better look. The deck came around and he could see the stairs Taylor was talking about. Michael noticed that one spot that he thought was a window was in fact a door. "Wow," he said as he turned his attention back to the room. The couch fit the room like a glove; like it was designed especially for the space. There was a TV in the room and another fireplace. He looked to his left and walked towards the kitchen. There was a tall island where the sink was and even a bar with stools on the island. The counter was long and stretched from one end of the wall to the other. He couldn't believe how big the house was.

Taylor who was seated on the couch said, "Well, let's go upstairs and then we will go down stairs." She jumped up and they followed. Michael grabbed Brittany's hand and kissed it. She smiled and they followed Taylor up the spiral stairs to another open space with a small couch and a table. To the right was a door and to the left was a door. Further down after you turned away from the stairs, was another door.

Taylor walked into the door on the right. It opened up to another bedroom that was about the same size as the first one they'd seen. It had a big bed and a chaise lounge instead of a couch. There was a window near the bed and some paintings on the wall. Taylor walked by them and back out to the open area. She went to the other doorway right across from the one they were in. That room was the biggest of all. It had an even bigger bed, a couch, and a reclining chair. Michael loved that room the most. Not because it was big but because he got the same warm feeling he did when he looked at the front room of the house.

Taylor walked to a door that was beside the bed and opened it. She walked out onto a porch. "This room has a small balcony on it. There are some chairs out here to enjoy the view." Michael could see nothing but tree tops and a few mountains trying to poke out from the trees.

Taylor closed the door and walked back to the open space. She turned and went to the last room upstairs. It was another bathroom. It was black and white and huge; the tub was heart shaped and had jets in it. The shower didn't have a door it was just open so Michael peered at a bench seat near the showerhead. *Nice!* Taylor opened a door that Michael thought was a closet and exposed a hidden toilet. *Talk about privacy!*

Taylor went out of the bathroom down the stairs to the bottom floor. Everyone kept in a line behind her. "Last but not least," she said. Michael was shocked by the room. It was the most open space in the house. There was a pool table in the middle of the room, a couch along one wall, a table along another with chairs, two massage chairs in a corner, and an arcade game by another wall. There were windows and a door facing the pool. The pool was big with a waterfall, slide, and diving board.

Michael watched Brittany walk over to the doors, open them, and walk outside. He followed behind her and closed the door after him. "Britt, thank you so much for planning this. It was sneaky and thoughtful of you. I love you and I just wanted you to know how happy this made me."

Brittany turned around and looked up at him. "Well I am very glad you like it. I admit that I had no idea it would be this amazing but I didn't really care where we went just as long as we did." Michael took her hand and they went to take a better look around the pool area. They walked over to the waterfall and slide. Michael saw something behind the waterfall and walked around to get a better look at what it was. It was a bar on wheels. It was around six-feet-long and four-feet-wide and decorated with straw and bead necklaces all over it. There were even stools that went with the bar. Michael walked around it and opened the doors under it. There was a ton of alcohol bottles stocked inside, glasses, and a small fridge. *Sure glad they stocked this too,* he thought as he and Brittany walked back inside.

They talked about who was staying in what room. It was Taylor's house so they insisted that she got first pick of her room. She decided she wanted the room downstairs with the bathroom attached in it; which was fine with Michael and Brittany because they wanted the room upstairs with the balcony attached to it. Michael took their luggage up to their room and Brittany followed. He was ready to be alone with Brittany so he could show her how happy he truly was.

# CHAPTER TWENTY-THREE

Brittany stepped into the room and took another look at how beautiful it really was. She couldn't get over everything in the house. From the rooms and decorations to the woods outside. The place was amazing. Michael laid the luggage on the floor and turned to face Brittany. He was so close that his nose was almost touching hers. She could feel his breath on her face and smell his cologne. She loved how he smelled.

Michael looked down into Brittany's eyes not saying a word. She held her breath feeling butterflies float through her. His gaze made Brittany hot and she couldn't take it anymore. In one swift motion she rushed her fingers to his face and pulled him in for a kiss. Before she knew it, his hands were on her waist pulling her even closer to him.

Her hands explored Michael's body slowly. She ran her hand down his chest to where his shirt ended. She pulled Michael's shirt off and stood back to admire his body. She never in this lifetime thought she would love a man with tattoos, but Michael's tattoos made him even sexier. She loved every inch of his body and could stare at it all day. However, at that moment, she didn't want to just stare. She wanted to explore every inch of his entire body.

In between her excitement, Brittany had a ping of guilt hit her in the heart. Michael was willing to show her all of him and she still hid behind a shirt. It wasn't right for her to hide from the person she loved. Michael took a step closer to her and before she could think she put her hand out to stop him. His face went blank and she was sure hers did to. Could she really do this? Could she really give her all to him? In her head, she could but her body just wasn't moving with her brain. It was something she had to do in order to show him just how much she loved him though. She held her breath and grabbed the bottom of her shirt. Closing her eyes she pulled her shirt off over her head. She dropped the shirt to the ground and kept her eyes closed. She just knew he would be looking at her scarred up mess of a stomach so she couldn't bear to look at him. She heard him step closer to her but not touch her. He never said a word and neither did she.

Time seemed to slow down and it felt like she was standing there for hours. Eventually, she felt his hot body close to hers. His breath was on her face. His hands stroked her face and he kissed her cheek that was wet. She didn't even know she was crying. She was so worried about what he would think that the tears that were running down her face were mute to her. She felt his mouth closer to her ear. "Britt, open your eyes." She heard him but she still didn't want to open them. A few minutes passed and she still kept her eyes closed. His mouth returned to her ear. "Britt, please look at me." She finally forced her eyes open and looked into his eyes.

She refused to speak, knowing she would fall apart if she did. "Britt, you have no idea how much that meant to me for you to do that. I want you to know that it only made me love you even more. Please listen to every word I am saying. I promise I am telling the truth. Your body was amazing before you let me see it all and now that I have seen it all it only turned me on more. I was hoping the day would come that you let me see all of you. You are more than perfect in my eyes." Michael ran his fingers over her stomach but never unlocked eyes with Brittany. "I love you inside and out. This part of you is not imperfect in my eyes. In my eyes, it's the best part of you. Think about it Britt. These show where you were in life and where you made it to. These scars are a part of you and I want every part of you to myself. I want to kiss every inch of you right now and that is just what I am going to do. No hiding from me anymore because you are mine and I am yours; all of you and all of me. Okay?"

Brittany felt another tear run down her cheek. She could only nod her head to him. Before she could wipe away the tear, Michael threw her on the bed and jumped on top of her. Her mind was racing and her heart pounding. *Did I hear him right? He actually loves me with the scars?* Michael kissed her hard and made her thoughts vanish in that moment. His hands explored her chest and stomach. Michael pulled back from her and sat up. Looking into Michael's eyes she suddenly saw raw passion and a hint of aggression in his eyes. Brittany felt herself squirm under his gaze awaiting his next move.

Michael got up off the bed and slid his pants and boxers off in one swift move; setting himself free. He was rock hard and wanting her badly. He walked to the bed, not taking his eyes off of hers. He leaned over her and reached for her pants. Still looking into her eyes, he jerked her pants off with a force that he never used before. Michael threw her pants on the floor and got back on top of Brittany. He placed soft kisses down her neck. Just when she thought he was going to place another kiss, he bit her instead. She jumped a little and moaned after the shock wore off. It did hurt a little but the pleasure from it was surprisingly overwhelming. He placed more soft kisses down to her chest.

With one hand, he roughly pulled the cup of her bra down and her breast fell out. Michael kissed her nipple then bit it. Again, she jumped, and moaned louder than the first time. The game he was playing was driving her crazy and she loved it. He moved over to the other breast and kissed and bit it as well. That time Brittany didn't jump and only moaned. Michael trailed kissed all the way down her stomach to the rim of her panties. At first Brittany was uncomfortable with it, but she soon let go. She could feel the stubble from his beard through the top of her panties and it made her squirm. "Be still Britt." Brittany immediately stopped moving. His tone of voice changed to one that was very demanding. It was rough and harsh but sexy at the same time. He was dominating her and she loved it. Michael ran his finger over her folds through her panties. Brittany could tell she was wet and her panties were now wet as well.

Before Brittany could think, Michael ripped the side of her panties and pulled what was left of them off. In a split second his mouth found her hot spot and Brittany lost control of her body. She was squirming and moving trying to get away from him. She knew she didn't want him to stop but the feeling was so intense that she couldn't control herself. "Michael please! Please, don't tease me! I want you now!" Michael stopped and looked up at Brittany; wiping his wet mouth with the back of his hand.

Michael slowly climbed up her body. Leaning down, he put his mouth close to her ear. "Britt, this is going to be fast and hard. If you want me to stop at all just say so, okay?" Brittany could only nod. Her body was going crazy and her mind couldn't keep up. She wanted and needed him so bad. Before she knew it, he rammed deep inside her, leaving her mind blank and breath gone.

***

Michael slid his boxers and pants back on and walked to the balcony. Brittany was wrapped up in the sheets fast asleep. He felt a slight breeze hit his body when he opened the door. *This place is wonderful,* he thought. But then again anywhere he was with Brittany was always wonderful. Michael couldn't help but think about what he and Brittany had just shared. He never expected her to show her stomach to him like that. He was happy that she did but was hurt by the look on her face when she did. Why couldn't she just understand that he loved her no matter what? That was why he was rough with her that time. He didn't want to just make love to her; he wanted her to understand that he was turned on because of what she did.

Michael looked out at the tree line and watched as the sun fell behind the trees. It was peaceful and quiet; just what he needed. It was the best day he had in a long time; other than the first night he really met Brittany. Michael had worked up an appetite so he decided to see what Mark and Taylor wanted to eat. Michael closed the doors and went to find his shirt. After kissing Brittany on the head he left her a note and tiptoed out the door and down the stairs.

Michael heard Taylor's giggle come from the living room. He stepped into the living room hoping he wasn't about to walk into something he didn't want to see. Thankfully he found Taylor laughing at something on TV with Mark sitting close next to her. Taylor turned her head to see Michael walk into the room. "Well hello lover boy. Where is the lover girl?"

Michael couldn't help but smile. "She is asleep. I came to see what y'all wanted for dinner tonight?"

Taylor looked back at the TV. "Well, I ordered pizza, from a little spot not too far from here. It should be here soon. I hope that's okay. I didn't want to interrupt what y'all had going on so I just went with something everyone should like."

Michael shrugged his shoulders and walked towards the kitchen. "That's fine with me and I'm sure Britt will be fine with that too."

Michael opened the fridge and pulled out a Pepsi. He

went to the door that led to the porch. Opening the door, he stepped out on the porch and went towards the hot tub. There was a cover over it but he could hear it running. He needed to make sure him and Brittany got a chance to relax in there later that night. He heard footsteps and turned to see Brittany walk out on the porch to where he was. He opened his arms and wrapped them around her.

"I'm surprised you're up."

"You know I don't sleep long when you're not with me."

Michael smiled and rested his chin on her head as they looked out over the porch to the pool.

Brittany pulled her head back and looked up at him. "Want to go swimming in the pool? It's heated and afterwards we can get in the hot tub."

Michael smiled down at her looking in her eyes. "Sounds good to me. Let's go change!"

Brittany started to lead the way and Michael reached out and lightly smacked her on the butt. She jumped and Michael couldn't help but laugh out loud. She only smiled and rolled her eyes walking into the house. With everything going wrong in their lives they seemed to find the best in it all.

# CHAPTER TWENTY-FOUR

T he mysterious man checked into a hotel not far from the house. Once he got settled into his room he made his way to the house. He'd found himself an area with thick bushes and trees. He positioned himself there with his binoculars. It was the best spot to see the back yard. He could see the porch, the pool, and the hot tub. Just when he was about to call it a day and head back to his hotel, he saw Michael step out onto a balcony. He wasn't wearing a shirt and was looking around. *Shit! Can he see me? No, there was no way he can see me. I'm hidden too well plus I have my camouflage on. That bastard isn't that smart anyway.* He made note it was more than likely the room Michael was staying in. He watched Michael walk back inside and waited for him to appear again.

A while later he saw some movement coming from the main level of the house. It was a guy and a girl; *must be Michael's idiot friends.* Before he left Virginia, he made plans to kill everyone in the house. In the end Michael would be to blame in the perfect murder suicide.

*** 

Brittany slid on her bathing suit bottoms. She picked up the two tops she had brought. One was a bra top and the other was a tight tank top. She decided to go all out and put on the bra top. Even though she felt that her scars ruined her stomach, it was flat for the most part. She figured it wouldn't be that bad because she was only swimming with

Michael plus, she brought a wrap to wear. Brittany pulled her hair back into a ponytail then tied the bikini top around her neck and back. She looked at herself in the mirror and then grabbed her wrap still not quite confident enough to go without it. Feeling better about herself, Brittany headed downstairs.

Mark and Taylor were in the kitchen making them each a plate of pizza. Brittany reached around Taylor and grabbed a plate. She put three slices of pizza on the plate and headed out the door. When she walked down the steps she saw Michael do a cannon ball off of the diving board into the pool. She moved to the bar, placed the plate on the bar, and walked around to the cooler to see what there was to drink. She decided to make them Tequila Sunrise when she saw there was a blender and everything else she would need for it stocked in the bar.

After blending up the ice and pouring the drinks she went back around the bar and found Michael sitting on the edge of the pool watching her every move.

"Come eat and have a drink."

He jumped up and pulled out a stool at the bar. After eating, Michael went back to the edge of the pool. "The water is as warm as bath water. Want to join me?" Brittany nodded and went to a lounge chair at the end of the pool. She took off her wrap. She went to the diving board and dove in head first. The rush of the warm water felt amazing on her skin. *Michael wasn't lying; the water does feel like bath water.* She surfaced the water and looked around for Michael. She spotted him swimming over to where she was.

"Well that was a much better dive then mine." Brittany giggled and splashed him in the face.

She swam as fast as she could to the end of the pool hoping he couldn't swim as fast as her. She reached the end of the pool and turned around to see where he was. It was too dark out to really see him at all. Just as she was looking for him, lights turned on around the pool. There were color changing lights on the inside of the pool around the edge and bright lights around the outside of the pool. She looked up to the house and saw Taylor and Mark heading down the stairs with their swim suits on. Michael jumped up out of the water in front of Brittany and she yelled. He scared the crap out of her but she laughed about it.

Taylor sat her stuff on the chair where Brittany's wrap was sitting.

"Y'all were out here in the dark. At first I thought y'all just wanted some privacy, but then I remembered that I forgot to tell y'all there were lights." Taylor laughed and went to the opposite side of the pool to where the slide was.

Mark dived off the diving board. As he jumped he slipped and did a belly flop. As he hit the water everyone said "ouch" and laughed. Mark came up for air and Michael said, "Dude, that shit had to hurt!" Mark splashed Michael and swam to the shallow end of the pool.

Taylor went down the slide and into the water. She surfaced and swam back to where Brittany was. "Hey let's play chicken!"

Mark nodded and Michael laughed. "I'm down. Let's do this."

Mark went under the water and Taylor got on his shoulders. Brittany couldn't help but laugh at them because Taylor almost fell. Michael went under the water and Brittany jumped on his shoulders. Michael lifted her out of the water and started to walk closer to Mark and Taylor. Taylor tried to push Brittany off and it almost worked until Brittany grabbed Taylor's hand and pushed really hard. Taylor went flying and fell off Mark's shoulders. Michael cheered and Brittany laughed. The rest of the night they played more pool games and had some drinks. Tired and wore out everyone went to bed. Brittany didn't even bother putting clothes back on after she took off her bathing suit. She just climbed in bed with Michael and fell asleep.

\*\*\*

The mysterious man eased his way up to the house and found a window. *Damn the blinds are closed on this one.* He found another window and looked in. The blinds were up on that one and he could tell it was a bedroom. *This must be where his friends are sleeping.* He made a mental note of the room's location and went to the front door. *I'll have to kill the friends first and then kill Mikey Boy and his bitch after.* The mysterious man was ready for it all to end. He was tired of dealing with all the shit and was ready to get on with his life. Once at the front door, he looked to see if he would be able to pick it. The lock seemed too hard to pick and he would possibly wake everyone up in the process. He'd already cut the power to the alarm in the breaker box on the side of the house but the clicking of the lock would cause a problem. He needed to find another door.

He followed the house to the back yard where the pool and deck were. There were two doors on the deck and one downstairs. He decided to go for the one under the porch. *Bingo! The idiots left it unlocked!* He slid the door open quietly and looked around for some stairs. After finding them he took one stair at a time as quietly as he could. His knife was drawn and he had a gun on his side. He wasn't planning on using the gun but had it just in case. He heard footsteps when he reached the top of the stairs. He froze on the last stair. He slowly backed down the stairs with his heart racing. He waited to see who it was. It was Michael coming down the stairs. He felt his heart pick up speed. *I need to kill Michael last but if that idiot comes down here I'll just have to kill him now.* Just when he thought Michael was coming in his direction he ended up turning and walking the other way. He hid, waiting until Michael went back to bed before he made his move. He had waited that long so a few more minutes wouldn't hurt. He crouched down low, not to be seen, and waited for his next move.

\*\*\*

Michael couldn't sleep; he had the old nightmare again. He grabbed his phone to use for a light to walked down stairs to get something to drink. Something felt off and he didn't know if it was just from the dream or what. Either way he wasn't going back to sleep. He pulled out a soda from the fridge, took a glance out the big windows, and headed back to his room. He didn't want to wake anyone else up so he decided to just hang out on the balcony for a little while. Michael got back into his room and opened one of the doors to the balcony. He sat down in a chair and listened to the quiet night. Taking a sip of his drink he realized he left his phone downstairs on the kitchen counter. He debated about if it was even worth it to go back and get it. He figured it was probably a good idea to get it; in case it rang he didn't want to wake anyone up. Michael sat his drink on the balcony ledge and headed back down the stairs.

Michael put one foot on the top of the stairs and froze. He saw a flash of a person walking towards Mark and Taylor's room. The person wasn't even walking. It was like they were creeping and crouched low to the ground. It was so quick Michael almost wondered if he was seeing things. Just when he was about to chop it all up to his mind playing tricks on him he heard a clicking noise. Someone was trying to pick the lock on Taylor's room. Michael backed up quietly and went back to his room where Brittany was. He quickly but quietly shook Brittany, hoping she would wake up. She finally did and Michael made a hand gesture for her to stay quiet. Brittany's eyes quickly got big and she mouthed "What?" to him. Michael leaned down and whispered in her ear. "Someone is in the house. I need you to get up and get dressed but be really quiet Britt." He could see her start to shake. Michael knew she would be terrified, especially after her prior encounter with the killer.

Brittany threw some shorts on and a tank top. Michael picked up her phone and dialed 911. He handed Brittany the phone and pointed towards the balcony. She must have read his mind because she walked out on the balcony and closed the door as quiet as she could. Michael looked around for some kind of weapon. He searched his bag and Brittany's bag. He found a pocket knife in Brittany's bag and a small bottle of hair spray. *This will have to work.* His heart was going crazy as he walked towards the door to their room. In one hand he had hair spray and the other he had the pocket knife. He had no clue if he was going to live or die but he damn sure was going to fight to protect his friends and the love of his life.

\*\*\*

CLICK. CLICK. CLICK. The door opened. The mysterious man could feel a bead of sweat run down his face as he looked over his shoulder to make sure no one was there. He briefly worried that he didn't give Michael enough time to go back to bed, but he didn't care anymore. He focused back on the door and slid it open just enough to ease his body in. He left the door cracked so he could get back out of it faster. In a crouching position, he made his way over to the bed. Mark was snoring and lying on the side where the door was at. He pulled out his knife and got closer to the bed. In one swift move, he pulled up the knife and rammed it down as hard as he could, not really caring where he hit.

Mark sat up as he pulled out his knife. The mysterious man looked him right in the face and smiled at him. Just as he was about to stab him again, Taylor rolled over and sat up. *Fuck!* She managed to scream before he could stab her too. He jumped on the bed over Mark, who was trying to roll off the bed to the floor. He used one hand to cover Taylor's mouth and the other to stab her in the leg. He held her face down to the bed and pulled the knife out of her leg. He had never felt more alive and in control then he did right then. He almost hated to end her life as fast as he was. He liked seeing her stupid face in so much pain and her eyes begging for him to stop. He pushed his knife into her side and her eyes closed. She either died or passed out. Either way, she wouldn't live long. He got off the bed and looked down at Mark lying in the floor in his blood. He wasn't moving so the mysterious man walked to the door. *Two down and two to go.*

He crouched down close to the floor again and opened the door, hoping that Taylor's scream didn't wake Michael or Brittany. He stood up and looked around not seeing anyone; he put the knife away in his pocket. *Now it is time for the gun.* He started to walk to the stairs and out of the corner of his eye he saw something move really fast. He couldn't tell what it was and before he knew it he was sprayed in his face and it burnt. *Fuck! Someone heard that whore scream after all.* He wiped his eyes and moved to see who it was. His vision was blurry but he could still make out that it was Michael.

***

Michael jumped out of the darkness as fast as he could. The man wasn't as quick as Michael was and when the man turned to face Michael, he sprayed him right in the eyes with the hairspray. Michael jumped back into the darkness and waited for the man to put up a fight. He wanted to know who this fucker was once and for all.

"Who are you and why are you trying to kill us?"

At first the man didn't move and didn't say anything.

Michael was starting to think the guy might try to run. This time he wouldn't get far, Michael was ready for that. The man smiled and looked Michael in the eyes. "You mean you truly don't remember?" Michael didn't say anything; he didn't know what to say. Of course, he didn't remember; if he did he wouldn't have asked. The man spoke again. "I'm going to tell you a little story Mikey Boy. Listen and listen well so you know every fucking detail." Michael watched the man's every move. He didn't want to give the guy a chance to come at him with a weapon. In the back of his mind, he knew the police would be here soon. He just hoped they would hurry because he didn't know if Mark and Taylor were okay.

"There was a small boy around five or six years old. He went with his dad to meet a friend of his. This friend owed the dad a serious amount of money and didn't want to pay the dad back. The dad didn't want to take the kid with him but the stupid mother said she needed a break from the bratty kid" Michael could feel his heart beating faster. He watched the guy stand up straighter and start to circle the room. Michael made sure to stay in front of him the whole time so he circled the room with him. He didn't want to give the guy any chance to get behind Michael.

"So, the dad was forced to take the kid with him. The dad drove out to a meadow where no one ever came to. Now pay attention Mikey Boy because this is where it gets good. The dad made the boy get out of the car in the cold weather. He wanted to show the kid how to handle people that didn't pay you back what they owe you. Friends or not, you just don't do that to people. So, the friend shows up and the dad gets into a fight with the friend. Anger fills the dad because the friend decided not to pay him back. He fights with his fist at first of course but soon he knows what he has to do. The friend thinks the fight is over and tries to walk away but he doesn't realize that the dad has picked up a sharp rock and followed the friend to his car. He takes the rock and hits the friend over the head as hard as he can. The friend falls down to the ground dying. The dad rolls the friend over and looks the bastard in the eyes. Want to know what the dad says to him?"

Michael still couldn't say anything, but he knew where this story was going. "Right before the friend takes his last breath the dad whispers to him. 'You should always pay your friends back. It's just business. You understand don't cha?' The dad gets up and starts to walk back to his truck. He suddenly realizes that his kid has watched the whole thing happen. The best part is that fucking kid is shaking on the ground and is rocking back and forth. The kid is out of his mind and the dad starts to really think about what to do. Want to know who the kid was?" The man stopped moving and smiled at Michael. "It was you, Michael. You want to know who I am? I am your dear old dad and you're my stupid bastard of a son. You see, I was going to kill you back then but I just didn't have the heart to do it. Looking back now it would have saved me so much time if I'd just done it then. I decided to let you live that day. I faked my own death and left town. I kept up with the news for a long time. Waiting to see if you would ever talk but you never did. Many years passed and I was about to just let it all go. Until I saw your picture in the papers saying how great of a football player you were and how you were going to go to college soon. It hit me then that you would eventually remember what happened that night and I would be hunted by everyone. So, I came back to make sure you kept your mouth shut."

Michael's gut felt like it had taken a beating. So many things still didn't make any since to him. "Why did you kill Ashley then?"

The man stopped smiling and looked down at the floor. "You see that didn't work out like I wanted it to. I killed her hoping you would be put in prison for the rest of your life. I had no idea the fucking idiot judge would only sentence you to eight years. I just wanted you in prison so you would keep your mouth shut. I never wanted to kill you but then when you got out and came to the rescue of your other little bitch; I had no choice but to kill you and your friends."

*Talk about fucked up parenting.*

Michael had heard enough. His hand tightened around the pocket knife and his teeth were clinched together. He had stalled as long as he could and the cops weren't there yet. He was angrier than ever. He had killed Ashley, tried to kill Brittany, and killed or seriously hurt his other two friends. He didn't deserve prison time, he deserved to die.

Seeing how angry Michael had become, the man said "Why don't we do this? I drop all my weapons and you do the same. We will fight like men."

Michael wasn't going to drop his weapon. "Yeah just like you did to your friend?" Michael finally heard sirens coming from outside.

The man smiled. "Well boy you didn't take money from me. You just wasted my whole life. Oh well, if you don't want to do it that way we can try another way."

The man pulled out his gun just as the cops kicked the door in. The man turned his head and looked to the door and Michael took it as his chance to strike. Michael jumped and shoved the man to the ground, knocking the gun out of his hand. When Michael jumped on the man, he rammed the knife as hard as he could in the man's chest. Michael could hear shouting from people behind him. A cop pulled him off of the man and pushed Michael up against a wall.

Brittany came down the stairs screaming something. The cop suddenly let go of Michael and rushed into Taylor and Mark's room. Michael looked over his shoulder and watched the cops try to stop the man's bleeding. He tuned into what the cops were saying only catching a few words. Something about stabbed in the heart and dead. That was all Michael needed to hear to help his mind come back to the present. Brittany was touching his face. "Are you hurt?" He shook his head. "The medics are in there with Taylor and Mark and won't let me in. I don't know what's going on Michael!"

Michael pulled Brittany close to him and kissed her forehead. "It's going to be okay Britt," he heard himself say the words but he really had no idea if it was going to be okay. He just hoped they weren't too late.

# CHAPTER TWENTY-FIVE
## Two Years later

Michael stepped out onto the back porch to the grill. He looked out at the yard where everyone was having a good time. It had been two years to the day since he came face to face with his dad. Even though the memories haunted him more often the he wanted, Michael was glad to have it all in the past. While Michael stood there flipping the burgers, he stepped back in time to that day for a second. That night seemed to go on and on forever. He thought of the moment he stood face to face with his so called "dad". His words stuck in Michael's head no matter how much he tried to shake it off. Michael managed to stab him in just the right spot to kill him almost instantly. If it wasn't for the cops breaking in the door and seeing his dad with a gun, then Michael might have been in trouble. Especially with him being an ex-con. Lucky for him the cops came just in time to see Michael defending himself. The cops eventually found his dad's house and what they found inside was disturbing. There were thousands of pictures all over every wall of Michael growing up. His dad was obsessed with him so bad that the cops concluded that he would have killed Michael in the end.

Mark and Taylor suffered major wounds and were transported to the local hospital. Mark got off easier then Taylor did, he only suffered one stab wound to the stomach and had to have part of his intestines taken out. Taylor on the other hand almost didn't make it. The stab wound to her leg caused her some nerve damage and the wound to her side punctured a lung and she lost a lot of blood. Luckily Brittany had the same blood type as Taylor and was able to donate blood for her.

Michael and Brittany spent the majority of their time at the hospital waiting for her to get out of the Intensive Care Unit. After almost two months of care Taylor was finally able to leave the hospital and go home to recover. Michael had moved in with Brittany by then so he helped Brittany take care of Taylor. She also had a therapist coming twice a week to help her regain mobility in her leg.

Mark was doing better and was able to convince Taylor to move in with him once her divorce was final. Brittany was a little heartbroken about it, but she was happy for her friend. Taylor and Mark made it a good habit to come over very often though. It took almost a year for things to finally smooth out and move in the right direction. Michael still to that day blamed himself for everything though.

Michael felt someone touch his side. He looked to see who it was. He smiled at the sight of Brittany. "Burgers will be done soon. Is everyone hungry?"

Brittany kissed him on the cheek. "Yes! We're starving. Just yell when it's ready, babe."

Michael watched her walk back off the porch. Seven months prior Michael was able to make Brittany his wife. He knew it wasn't great timing when he asked her to marry him, but she said yes anyway. Michael smiled at that memory. Brittany was helping Taylor move her stuff into Mark's house; she was sweating and irritated to say the least. She had just brought in the last box of Taylor's things and sat it down. When she turned around to walk back out the door Michael was on one knee with the ring out. That was the most nerve racking thing he'd ever done. His heart told him she would say yes but worry still lingered as well. She said yes and they got married right in Brittany's back yard in the presence of her dad, his mom, Mark, Taylor, Mark's mom, and Taylor's parents. It was simple and that's what they both wanted. As Michael looked at Brittany, he couldn't picture their life any other way.

Michael's mom was so happy for him on his wedding day that she cried. As for Brittany's dad, it took a little time for him to accept that Michael wasn't going anywhere. Michael always said it would be hard for Officer Johnson to let go of the fact that he was wrong about Michael. Surprisingly it wasn't as hard for Michael to forgive him as he thought, because he had Brittany. Now two years later, Michael's record was expunged, and Officer Johnson finally decided to let go of his pride and could see that Michael was one of the good guys.

With Brittany's help, Michael went back to school and took up Criminal Justice. He worked hard in school and graduated at the top of the class. Finding a job wasn't as hard as he figured it would be. Officer Johnson retired one month after Michael graduated from school and Michael took his job on the force. Still to that day Michael felt that he only left so Michael could join the squad. Officer Johnson would never admit it though, so it was one thing he would never know for sure. One thing he did know for sure was the burgers were ready and his family and friends were hungry. He turned the grill off and placed the burgers on the plate.

Walking to the table on the porch, he yelled for everyone to come eat. He watched as everyone gathered around the table with him. Mark helped Taylor walk up the steps and to the table. She still had a little limp so moving fast was still hard to do but she managed to get better and better with time. Brittany stood on one side of Michael and Jenny on his other side. Johnson stepped in beside Brittany while Mark and Taylor filed in beside him. In a circle around the table Michael asked everyone to join hands. "It's been two years since we all went through the worst time of our lives and yet here we are standing strong. We have stayed by each other's sides through it all and came out on top. I am grateful to have each and every one of you in my life more then you will ever know. So, let's celebrate making it as far as we have because we damn well deserve it." Everyone laughed and shook their heads.

Mark grabbed a plate off the table. "Okay dude, if you're done with your sappy speech we are starving and would like to eat now!" Everyone laughed again, started to grab their plates, and made their way around the table. Michael could only smile because he finally had the perfect life he always wanted. Even with the bumps along the way, they finally got to where they all should be. To Michael, that was a happy ending.

# FRAMED 2
## Preview...

Jennifer waited on her last customer to finish looking around. It had been a long day and she was ready to get home. She spent all her time at the shop and some days it paid off, others it didn't. She remembered when she bought the shop three years prior. She always loved clothes and fashion and people in this small town could really use it. It took all her savings to buy the place but it was something she loved so she was okay with it. Now three years later she made enough to keep the bills paid and have a little extra cash to save away.

Looking off in the distance, Jennifer began to think of her sister. Tiffany loved fashion just as much as she did. It had been well over six years since she had talked to Tiffany. Tiffany was the only family that Jennifer had but she did not care if they had each other or not. She couldn't really blame Tiffany though. They had been through so much growing up, but always stuck by each other's sides; from foster care at age twelve to getting their first place together. It was a bad life that finally started to get better, until Jennifer messed it up. She couldn't be mad at the fact that Tiffany was mad for what she did, but did she really have to still hate her after six years? Every year Jennifer would call Tiffany on Christmas morning but she would never answer the phone. So, Jennifer just left the same message on the machine hoping her sister would pick up the phone. She never did, but Jennifer wouldn't stop trying. She would make the call again that year and say the same thing as always but she didn't count on her sister picking up the phone.

Jennifer looked at the clock to check the time. She tried to close the shop by nine every night. It was nine-thirty. The woman seemed to be looking for something so Jennifer decided to give her another five minutes before she told her that she was going to have to close. She hadn't ever seen this woman before and Jennifer rarely ever saw new people come in the shop. Regulars loved her store and from time to time she would get a new person but they were always passing through. Jennifer decided to get the till counted out and put away. If the lady bought something Jennifer would just get change out of the bag and add it in once she got home. Her night would be the same as any other night. A short walk home to her apartment, sitting on the couch with her cat, Missy, and doing the store's paperwork from the day's sales. *My life is pretty boring. Maybe I should try going on a date or something. Nah.* Her friend Alexis tried to set her up on a blind date and it blew up into a fat ball of nothing. At twenty-seven years old, she should have a boyfriend, but no one seemed to strike her in any way that she cared to progress.

Putting the money in the bag and closing the till, Jennifer looked at her clock for the time again. It was nine-forty and time to close up the shop. "Ma'am I'm sorry but the store is going to have to close. We are open tomorrow from nine am to nine pm if you would like to come back." The woman didn't look at Jennifer. She just walked to the door and left. *Well, that was weird.* Jennifer didn't mean to upset the woman but it was already forty minutes after closing time. *Oh well.* Jennifer went to the back of the store and grabbed her purse and jacket. It was winter time in Virginia and that meant snow and wind. It was a short walk home but it didn't take much to make Jennifer cold.

Jennifer cut off the lights and headed to the front door. Locking the door behind her, she put her keys and phone in her purse. Town was really quiet at that time of night, especially on a Tuesday. She looked around and didn't see a car on the street at all. It was starting to snow again so she hurried down the sidewalk. She was thankful the city kept the sidewalks pretty clean. There was already a few inches on the ground from the snow storm that came the day before. Folding her arms over each other, she stopped at the light to wait for the hand to signal her to walk. It seemed stupid to stand and wait so she hurried across the road. She could see a street light out not far down the road.

Jennifer got a cold chill that ran up her spine and made her shiver. She suddenly had a bad feeling come over her. "Oh, get a grip Jennifer. You watch way too many scary movies." She pulled her arms closer to her body and kept walking. Once at the street light, she heard a strange noise. There was a girl sitting on the ground by a dumpster in the alley way crying. *How odd.* She almost kept walking but then she wouldn't want someone to do that if it was her. Jennifer didn't really want to go down the alley way so she just figured she would yell out to her. "Are you okay over there?" She waited for an answer but the girl was crying so loud that she must not have heard Jennifer.

Slowly Jennifer walked down the alley trying to get a better view of the girl. She couldn't get a good look at the girl's face because her hood was pulled down over her head and she was sitting with her knees to her chest. Once she was about a foot away from her she asked her again, "Are you okay?" The girl stopped crying but didn't move. Jennifer had a strong feeling in her gut to run, but she stood there waiting for the girl to say something or at least move. Suddenly the girl jumped up and shoved Jennifer against the wall. Jennifer hit her head hard on the bricks and almost passed out. "If it's money you want, you can have it. It's in my purse. Here just take it." Jennifer tried to pull her arm free to hand the girl the purse but her grip was too tight on Jennifer's arm.

"I don't want your money, bitch!" The girls voice was almost hoarse and rough sounding. Before Jennifer could fight back, the girl rammed a knife into Jennifer's leg. Jennifer tried to scream but the girl must have known she would because she put her hand over Jennifer's mouth. Jennifer's brain was telling her to fight like hell but her body was hurting so bad. She pushed the girl as hard as she could and lucky for her the girl stumbled just a little. That was Jennifer's chance and she knew it. Jennifer used her good leg and rammed it into the girl's stomach. The girl let go of Jennifer long enough for her to run. With every step her leg grew more and more painful. Biting her tongue, she gave it every ounce of energy she had, but it wasn't enough. The girl caught up with Jennifer and stabbed her in her shoulder. Jennifer fell to the ground, knowing it was over. Her body was going numb and the pain was leaving her body fast. The girl rolled Jennifer over and sat on top of her. Jennifer couldn't say a word. She just watched the girl and waited for the end. The girl pulled off her hood and smiled down at Jennifer. In one swift move, she jammed the knife into Jennifer's chest. Looking into the stranger's eyes, Jennifer took her last breath.

# ACKNOWLEDGMENTS

Writing has always been a hidden passion of mine that I was never able to uncover. That was until I found my beautiful and amazing publisher, Sharona Seigler. She helped guide my pen to the paper and bring you my stories. She also kept my spirits lifted and my confidence in check. I will never be able to thank her enough. I also need give a special thanks to Cedric Lewis and Jamie Shell. Without them I would have never gotten in touch with my publisher and my dreams would never have come true.

I also want to thank my mother Charlie Johnson. She is the one who had me fall in love with reading at an early age. To this day my mother loves to read and she was my inspiration to write. Without fail I can ask my mother what the best book out is and she will eagerly share the title(s). I hope one day when I ask her she will say it's mine. You are such a strong mother, wife, sister, daughter, and the list goes on. I have learned so many things from you and I am so grateful to have you in my life. I love you Mom!

Another thank you goes out to my amazing number one fan and fiancé Michael Rio. You were the one who told me to write my own book when I couldn't find one to read. You have been there through it all and I am so lucky to have you by my side. Thank you for all of your support and encouraging words when I needed it most. Thank you to my three beautiful children Eli, Shyann, and Alana. You are what keeps me going every day of my life. Eli, you always give the best hugs and make my bad days so much better. Shyann, you know how to make me laugh every day, either by your clumsiness or your silliness. Alana, you have given me so much love in my heart from your beautiful smile to your heart warming laugh. I love you all very much.

Last but not least, thank you to all my new fans. My dream is to write books that take you to a new place and help you escape life for a brief time. I hope my books bring you as much joy reading them as they do me writing them. Thank you for your support.

www.ingramcontent.com/pod-product-compliance
Lightning Source LLC
Chambersburg PA
CBHW061521020726

47502CB00006B/2174